Menace in the Fog

MENACE
IN THE
FOG

J. H. Rhodes

AVALON BOOKS
THOMAS BOUREGY AND COMPANY, INC.
22 EAST 60TH STREET • NEW YORK 10022

Menace in the Fog

CHAPTER ONE

Janis Long took one hand off the steering wheel and brushed a strand of wheat-colored hair away from her eyes. Now that she had entered the state of Oregon, she felt herself beginning to relax. The trip across the country from New York had been a frantic one and she felt the muscles in her shoulders begin to ache, more from tension than from exertion.

She had gotten an early start today and from her calculations she reckoned that she should be at Winter House by nightfall.

Winter House. The name intrigued Janis. Her turquoise-blue eyes took in the Oregon countryside as she thought about Clifford Green. Winter House belonged to Clifford, not to mention a home in Florida, a villa in the south of France, and an apartment in New York. She wasn't certain how Clifford Green had arrived at

1

the name Winter House, but he had merely shrugged
when Janis had asked him and had said something
flippant about how he had a summer house and it stood
to reason that there had to be a Winter House.

It had been Clifford who had suggested she stay at
Winter House for a while, at least until she had finished
her illustrations for the new Elyse book. At the time
the offer had seemed like an answer to Janis's prayers.
Things were not going well with herself and Floyd
Phillips.

Thinking of Floyd, she felt a slight chill tingle her
spine. As far as Janis was concerned, she had never
been serious about him. She had made that clear when
they had met. At first Floyd had been content with the
relationship and then he had changed. The lightness
had gone out of their friendship and he had become
suspicious and jealous of her.

The night before she left New York, there had been
a showdown. Janis had told Floyd that she didn't think
they should see each other again.

"You can't mean that," Floyd had said across the
table in the restaurant. The restaurant Janis had chosen
so as to be safe. "You'll change your mind once you
get back from Oregon."

But Janis had been firm. "No, Floyd. I could never
feel for you what you feel for me. I think of you just
as a friend."

A dark scowl spread itself across Floyd's face.
"There's somebody else, isn't there?"

"Of course not," Janis said, becoming uneasy. "I'm
just going to Oregon to do the illustrations for the new
book. Mr. Green thought I might be able to use Winter
House as a setting for Elyse's new adventures."

"You've been seeing a lot of Clifford Green."

"He publishes the books I illustrate," Janis said in a calm, level voice.

"I don't like the man. He's turned you against me." Floyd's voice was heavy with venom.

"That's just plain silly," Janis said. "Clifford Green is a much older man. And he's a very thoughtful person to work with."

The scowl deepened on Floyd's face. "There hadn't better be anyone else. I'm warning you, Janis. You belong to me. If there is anyone else, you'll be sorry."

Janis had stared at Floyd in disbelief. She couldn't understand the man. Had he really threatened her? She had left the table then, grabbing her purse and hurrying out of the restaurant. Janis had taken a taxi home, not caring to see Floyd again.

The telephone had rung when she arrived at her apartment, and it had been Floyd. From the moment she had answered, he had ranted and raved until she was forced to hang up on him. Then the phone continued to ring, but she refused to pick it up.

After packing her things in her small car, Janis had fled New York. She kept thinking of Floyd and the threats he had made. By the end of the third day on the road, Janis found that she was thinking less and less of Floyd and looking forward to living in Oregon for however long it took her to complete the illustrations for the new book.

Janis had drifted into illustrating juvenile books purely by accident. She had been spending the weekend at her parents' home in Maine and had brought some of her artwork with her. There had been a guest that weekend, Alice Martin, an editor at the Green Publishing Company. Urged on by her mother, Janis had shown the woman her work. The editor had been impressed by Janis's talent and had later contacted her, asking if she would be interested in illustrating a new series of books with a young girl named Elyse as the heroine. Alice Martin described Elyse and the first book in the series.

Janis had sent the editor some sketches showing how she pictured Elyse, and then she had been asked to do the illustrations for the book. The first book had been well-received, and the illustrations were praised. After that, Janis had been commissioned to do the whole series on Elyse, working closely with the author, an ex-schoolteacher.

Somehow during this period, Floyd Phillips had drifted into Janis's life. Being alone in New York, Janis had welcomed him as a new friend. Unfortunately, that was not what Floyd had in mind.

Janis sighed now as she concentrated on the road ahead. She turned on the radio and let the music swell around her as she continued toward her destination. Once she glanced into the rearview mirror and saw the faint shadows that had formed beneath her blue eyes. Outside of that, there was little to indicate her recent lack of sleep. Janis was usually a cheerful, breezy person. It was only this unhappy relationship with Floyd that had lately dampened her spirits.

As the car hummed along the highway, Janis suddenly thought about yesterday and the motel where she had spent a rather restless night. It was after dark when she had arrived and, after checking in and eating at the restaurant that was connected to the motel, she had returned to her room. It was just as she was inserting her key in the lock that she had felt the presence of someone across the court staring at her.

Janis had slowly turned and, as she did, the man across the court had stepped into the shadows. An icy chill had coursed its way down her back because she thought the man she had seen was Floyd Phillips. Without hesitating, Janis hurried into the room and quickly shut the door behind her. She leaned against the door for a few moments, thinking about what she had seen. Had she been mistaken? Had she just thought she had seen Floyd standing across the court from her?

It was an endless night with Janis trying desperately to get to sleep but tossing and turning, afraid that if that man had been Floyd, he just might try something. When she finally did manage to get to sleep, her dreams turned into hideous nightmares about Floyd and dark passageways that she frantically ran through.

When Janis awoke the next morning, she felt as though she had not slept at all. But after taking a brisk, cold shower and having some breakfast, she felt better. As she went to her car, she glanced furtively around, but she did not see Floyd Phillips, just some other people who were staying at the motel. Even so, she felt that Floyd might be spying on her from some window in the motel. Janis had to give herself a good dressing down in order to regain her perspective.

Leaving the motel, she glanced occasionally into the rearview mirror, but no car appeared to be following her, just the usual flow of traffic. She had switched on the car radio and felt herself being enveloped by the sweep of music. When she found herself humming along with one particular song, she became convinced that she had almost shaken off the frightening experience of the night before.

At noon she stopped for lunch at a hamburger place in a small town. She felt content as she munched on the delicious hamburger and took occasional sips of hot, steaming coffee. Here, in this cozy, friendly atmosphere, it seemed almost impossible that Floyd Phillips could be anywhere nearby. In fact, Janis felt that he was still hundreds of miles away in New York. How foolish she had been in thinking that he would follow her all the way to Oregon. Yet, even as she tried to reassure herself, niggling doubts began to taunt her.

After she had finished eating, Janis put her dog-eared road map on the table and studied it for what seemed the hundredth time. At the rate she was traveling, she should be at Winter House by nightfall. She was glad that she was nearing her destination and that she had her work to do.

The little girl named Elyse had almost become a real person to Janis after the many months she had spent bringing her to life on her sketch pad. The latest adventure, a mystery story, was the best that had been written about the inquisitive and spunky little girl.

Janis couldn't help but smile as she thought how Elyse would look in the new book. Her artistic nature had taken over from the day she had received the text of the new book. She ate, thought, and slept with ideas whenever there was a new Elyse story. The little girl simply seemed to take over Janis and show her how she would look and behave in certain situations. Winter House, according to Clifford Green, would be the perfect setting to turn Elyse loose in.

"Feel free to use any of the furnishings and paintings in your illustrations," Clifford had told Janis before she had left New York. "They are all authentic. And they are all expensive."

Janis did not doubt for a minute that Clifford Green spoke the truth. He was a meticulous, precise person whose taste in practically everything was impeccable. Yet, in spite of all this, he was a warm, caring man.

Janis had learned that Clifford's wife had died some years before. He had a son, Lucas, whom he rarely spoke of. Janis had the feeling that Clifford might be just a little disappointed in his only child, but she had no way to verify this. Lucas would be at Winter House along with another guest. It seemed that people were always dropping in for shorter or longer stays at any of Clifford Green's many residences.

Taking the map, Janis returned to the car and drove away, giving a fond wave to the man and his wife who ran the small hamburger place. Oregon was certainly a state of contrasting scenery, of valleys and mountains and peace.

Towards sunset Janis found herself nearing the place on the coast known as Call's Bay. She breathed in the tangy smell of seawater and for a moment she thought about the East Coast and the summer vacations at the beach. But as she looked around, she was reassured by the passing scenery that she was in Oregon and not in Maine or any other eastern seaboard state.

The farther Janis drove, the more she became aware of the gauzy fog that was beginning to surround the car and blanket the highway. She slackened her speed as she maneuvered the car around the serpentine curves of the road.

The fog thickened as she drove at what seemed to her an ant's crawl. There was little traffic on the road and Janis was thankful for that. Each mile that brought her nearer to Winter House brought thicker fog. As Janis drew close to her destination, she turned off on a side road although she did not see the sign she was looking for. In the distance, though, she could see the yellowish glimmer of lights and she felt that she had been right to turn off at this road.

As Janis neared the source of the lights, she saw a house looming through the fog. Now she wondered if the place was Winter House, after all. It in no way resembled what she had been told by Clifford Green.

Braking the car, Janis got out and walked toward the house. It was a long wooden structure with a wide porch. No sooner had Janis taken a step on the wooden floor of the porch than the front door was suddenly thrown open.

A gruff male voice said, "What are you doing here? Don't you know this is private property?"

Janis stared at the man who stood before her. He was tall. His wide shoulders filled the doorway, and the muscles of his chest strained against his shirt buttons. His dark-brown eyes seemed to bore into Janis from beneath his shaggy eyebrows.

At a glance, Janis assessed that he was what might be termed ruggedly handsome. But at the moment she was too annoyed at his rude behavior to pay any attention to that.

"Is this Winter House? I'm Janis Long and I'm expected," she said, trying to keep the anger from her voice.

"Winter House? You've taken a wrong turn," came

the sarcastic reply. "You must not be a very alert driver."

This last remark was uncalled for and Janis had taken about all she could. "Who could be alert in all that fog? I just lost my way, that's all. You certainly aren't very hospitable, Mr. . . ."

"Roark, Tim Roark," he said.

"Well, Mr. Roark, if you'd be so kind as to tell me how to reach Winter House, I'd appreciate it. Or is that straining your hospitality?"

"Not in the least," Tim Roark said in an amused tone of voice, which only infuriated Janis all the more. "You were on the right road until you took this side road. Just go back to the highway. Winter House is about a mile up the highway. Do you think you can find your way now?"

"There isn't any doubt in my mind that I can," Janis said. "And thanks for all the trouble."

"No trouble. I'll be seeing you again, Janis Long."

"I doubt that," she said.

Tim Roark chuckled. "Don't be sure about that. I'm a regular visitor to Winter House. Clifford even gave me a key."

"I hope I know when you're arriving so I can avoid seeing you," Janis said as she turned angrily and walked back to the car.

CHAPTER TWO

As Janis's hand touched the handle on the car door, she felt a presence behind her, and she turned to see Tim Roark standing there. He had followed her from the house.

"Just want to make certain you made it to your car, all right," Tim said. "The fog is getting thicker and I didn't want you to get lost."

Janis wished that the fog would lift for a moment so that she could scrutinize Tim's face. She had no way of telling in this heavy mist whether or not he was making fun of her.

"Thank you," Janis said with as much warmth as she could muster at the moment. "I wasn't worried about finding my car as much as I'm concerned about getting to Winter House. The fog can be very deceptive."

"Yes, it can be," Tim replied in an even tone of voice. "But if you follow my instructions, I doubt you'll have any problems."

Janis opened the door to her car and got behind the steering wheel.

Then before she could turn the key in the ignition, Tim said, "I hope that you turn out some good illustrations while you're at the house, Miss Long."

"How did you know about that?" Janis asked, peering through the veil of fog at Tim Roark.

"You're in the country, Miss Long," Tim said. "And news travels fast around here."

Janis turned the key in the ignition and the engine came to life. She turned her head back to where Tim Roark had been standing, but he was no longer there. Janis stepped on the accelerator and drove away from the house.

As she slowly rode through the fog, she thought about her encounter with Tim Roark and how rude he had been. Up to a point, that is. He had walked her to her car, which did show that he wasn't entirely without consideration. Or had he just been curious about her?

"You're just letting this fog get to you," Janis said aloud, and the sound of her voice brought reassurance to her.

Sure, Tim Roark was curious. Why shouldn't he be? A perfect stranger comes wandering onto his property at sundown . . . Who wouldn't be curious? Still, Tim Roark seemed to know something about her, that she was an artist. Just how much did he know about her?

Janis reached the highway and continued her journey. Straining her eyes, she soon saw a house standing off to her right. She could see a turnoff that led to the house and she knew that this time she had found Winter House. A small sign confirmed this. Janis gave a sigh of relief as her foot pressed down on the gas pedal with new urgency. She would be glad to get to her destination. The cross-country drive was beginning to take its toll on her.

Turning onto the gravelly side road, Janice could see that Winter House, perched high on a hill, was a three-storied structure. Its warm, cheery lights cut through the gray fog.

The nearer Janis got to the house, the more excited she became. From all that she had dimly seen of the place, it would be perfect for the new Elyse book. Her weariness began to vanish as she looked forward to seeing Clifford Green's home.

Janis parked the car before one of the three garages whose doors were tightly closed. It was only then that she became aware of another car, one that had been following her ever since she'd left the residence of Tim Roark. The car came to a halt beside her and the engine was still idling.

"Just wanted to make certain that you didn't get lost again," came the deeply masculine voice of Tim Roark. "But I see that you arrived safe and sound."

There was a mocking tone to his voice that irritated Janis somewhat. But she did not want Tim Roark to know that his presence disturbed her in the least.

"Thank you for your concern," Janis said in a level tone of voice. "Is escorting one of your services?"

That remark brought a laugh from Tim Roark. It was an infectious sound and Janis found herself actually smiling at the man who only a short while ago had irritated her.

"If all newcomers were as charming as you, then I wouldn't mind escorting them. Well, now that you're here unharmed, I'll be getting back to my home. Take care, Janis Long."

With that, Tim expertly made a turn in the driveway and was gone in the swirling fog. For an instant, Janis felt a slight lump in her throat. There was a charm about Tim Roark that both attracted and annoyed her.

She sighed and walked toward the house. What she did not need at this time in her life was another relationship. Then Janis realized how ridiculous that thought was. After all, she had just met Tim Roark.

Janis climbed the few flagstone steps to a small alcove. For a moment she stared at the heavy oaken door wondering what lay beyond it. Then she lifted the heavy old-fashioned knocker and let it fall back into place.

It seemed an eternity before the door opened and she found herself staring into the hazel eyes of a tall brunette woman about her own age.

"You must be Janis," the woman said in a remote tone of voice. "Clifford said that you would be coming."

"Yes, I'm Janis. I would have been here sooner, but I took a wrong turn. I'm afraid I'm not used to your Oregon country yet," Janis said, feeling uneasy under the unblinking gaze of the woman.

"Please come in," the woman said. "I'm Dolores Webster."

"Are you one of the help?" Janis asked.

The hazel eyes narrowed in icy anger. "Of course, not. Clifford Green is a dear friend of my father. I'm a guest here at Winter House. Just as you are."

Janis realized that she had inadvertently made an enemy of Dolores Webster. But she felt that there would be time to remedy that.

"I have a few things in the car . . ." Janis said.

"They'll be brought in," was Dolores's cool reply. "Are you planning on staying long?"

It really was no concern of Dolores Webster's, but Janis did not wish to antagonize the woman further.

"Just until I finish the new book. However long that will take."

"Oh, that's right," Dolores said. "You do pictures for those silly children's books."

If she stayed in that house for fifty years, Janis knew that she and Dolores would never get along. "They sell quite well. And Clifford seems to like them. Otherwise, I'm sure he wouldn't publish them. But then everyone doesn't have Clifford Green's taste."

"I'll see if I can find Winnifred. She'll show you to your room," Dolores replied as she pivoted and walked briskly away, leaving Janis alone in the strange hall.

Now that she was by herself, Janis glanced around at her surroundings. She was in a long, shadowy corridor lighted by wall sconces that gave off very little light. The main stairway was quite impressive. There were a few oil paintings on the walls and at a quick glance Janis recognized the work of some modern artists.

In the center of the corridor were open doors that obviously led to the downstairs rooms.

A door on the right opened and Janis saw a rather

heavyset, squat woman with short-clipped gray-streaked hair emerge. When she saw Janis, she smiled warmly. Janis could not help smiling back. Whoever this woman was, she was certainly the most friendly person she had met since coming to Oregon.

"Miss Long, I'm Winnifred," the woman said as she advanced towards Janis, wiping her hands on her apron.

Janis extended her hand and the woman took it with a firm and friendly grasp.

"I'm pleased to meet you, Winnifred," Janis said and she meant every word.

"Miss Dolores told me you were here and I just had to meet you. My grandchildren just love those Elyse books. Whenever I baby-sit for my older daughter, they have me read the books over and over to them."

"Thank you, Winnifred. That kind of news makes my work worthwhile," Janis said.

"Mr. Green told me you were coming and I've been excited ever since. Have you had your supper?"

"Well, no. I did stop for something around lunchtime," Janis said.

"Come along to the kitchen," Winnifred said with a wave of her hand. "You don't mind eating in the kitchen, do you?"

"Not in the least," Janis said as she followed the squat woman down the corridor.

The kitchen was located to the right of the corridor. It was a warm, comfortable place, and the aroma of fresh-brewed coffee hung in the air.

"Why don't you sit down and I'll bring you a cup of coffee first," Winnifred said, nodding toward a small table standing by a window.

After Janis had taken a seat, she realized that she

had been sitting for what seemed years behind the wheel of her car, and now here she was sitting down once more.

Opposite her, Winnifred was busily fixing a sandwich for her. It was obvious that Winnifred felt right at home in the huge, three-storied house. Janis idly wondered how long the woman had been at Winter House.

Almost as though Winnifred sensed what Janis was thinking, she said, "I've been with Mr. Green for about five years. Since he first bought the house. My husband had just died. At first it was just me and another person working here. After that, Mary Lee and Jonas joined us. Now it's the three of us and we all get along just great."

"Who are Mary Lee and Jonas?"

"Mary Lee's my younger daughter. She's about your age. She and me handle the household duties. Jonas is the gardener. He's a quiet one, almost surly, but he does his job real well."

Having said that, Winnifred brought Janis her food. As Janis munched on the roast-beef sandwich and sipped her coffee, Winnifred poured herself a cup and brought the hot, steaming liquid to the table.

"Do you mind if I sit with you?" the housekeeper asked.

"Of course, not," Janis said. "I'd enjoy the company."

That was all that Winnifred needed. She plopped her ample self down in a chair opposite Janis and said, "I really hope that you like staying here, Miss Long. It really is a nice home and Mr. Green has such priceless things in it. Kinda makes me nervous sometimes, thinking about how much money he's paid for all those paintings and furniture."

"Please call me Janis. Miss Long is just too formal for me. I'm not the formal type."

Winnifred brightened at that remark. "I just knew you were natural and down-to-earth. It shows in those books of yours."

"But all I did were the pictures."

"They tell just as much as the words, as far as I'm concerned," Winnifred said with a quick, brisk smile. "This place needs someone like you right about now."

Janis studied Winnifred for a moment. She wondered if the woman was indulging in idle chatter. But there were slight worry lines between Winnifred's eyebrows.

"Is there anything wrong here at Winter House?" Janis asked, taking a quick sip of her coffee.

Winnifred slowly shook her head. "Not wrong, exactly. It's just something I can't put into words. Just a feeling I have. And you know what feelings are."

Janis thought she understood what the heavyset housekeeper was getting at, but she didn't know quite what to say.

"How long have you had these feelings?" Janis finally said.

"Just within the past several months. Right after Lucas arrived and Miss Webster came for her annual visit."

"I haven't met Lucas. Is he home?"

"Most likely he's off on one of his walks. He likes to get off by himself. He's not a bit like his father. Mr. Green is very friendly and hospitable. Lucas is

very quiet and withdrawn. They couldn't be more un-
like in temperament. Still Lucas is quite likable in his
way."

At that moment, they were interrupted by a pretty
young girl whom Winnifred introduced as Mary Lee.
The three chatted for a few minutes. And when Janis
had finished eating, Winnifred suggested that Mary Lee
take Janis to her room.

Mary Lee guided Janis through the corridor to the
stairs and she was almost as animated as her mother.
It was very apparent that both Mary Lee and her mother
enjoyed their work here at Winter House.

Janis's room was on the second floor and the last
room on the left. They passed by several doors and
Mary Lee pointed out who had which bedroom. Lucas
Green, whom Janis hadn't yet met, had the first bedroom and Dolores occupied the bedroom between Janis
and Lucas. That left three opposite bedrooms unoc-
cupied. The servants, apparently, slept on the third
floor.

When they arrived at Janis's bedroom, Mary Lee
opened the door with what appeared to be great plea-
sure. Janis stepped inside and saw a lovely wallpapered
room with a canopied bed standing at the far wall
between two windows.

"Do you like it?" Mary Lee asked needlessly.

"It's lovely. It even has a huge desk where I can do
my artwork."

Mary Lee seemed pleased that Janis was so happy.
She chatted away as Janis walked about the spacious
room, coming to a Sheraton chest of drawers. She
couldn't be certain that it was actually a Sheraton piece
because she actually did not know that much about

antiques. But it did look quite old and in excellent condition. The only jarring thing about the chest of drawers was the black cassette player that lay on the crocheted doily.

As Mary Lee kept talking, Janis touched the cassette player. She had absently pushed one of the buttons as she listened to Mary Lee. Winnifred's daughter suddenly stopped talking and another voice, a disguised one, filled the room. Janis and Mary Lee turned their attention to the cassette player, for the voice came from there.

"You, Janis Long, are an unwelcomed guest here at Winter House. This is a warning to you. Leave now while you still can. There's danger here at Winter House. Danger for you."

CHAPTER THREE

The voice died, but the tape cassette continued to turn. Janis reached out and touched the off button, and the room was pitched into silence.

"That's terrible," Mary Lee said, her eyes wide with fright.

"It must be a practical joke," Janis said in an effort to put Mary Lee at ease.

"Some joke," Mary Lee said as she put her hands on her slim hips. "If you ask me, whoever left that thing here has a sick mind."

"Do you recognize the cassette player?" Janis asked.

Mary Lee walked over to the chest and stared at the player for a moment or two. She slowly shook her head. "I've never seen it before. It looks brand new. I wonder how it got here."

"Well, I've always wanted one of these things,"

Janis said as she picked up the player and put it into one of the drawers.

Mary Lee edged toward the door and, before she left, she said, "If you need me, just call. And I'll come running."

Janis smiled at the frowning girl. Mary Lee was obviously worried about her, and Janis did not want the girl to be unduly concerned.

"I'll be just fine, Mary Lee. But if I do need anything, I'll call. Okay?"

The frown lines quickly faded from Mary Lee's face and she smiled back at Janis. "Okay. I'm really glad that you came to Winter House, Miss Long."

"Janis, please."

"See you, Janis."

After Mary Lee had gone, Janis gazed around the room once more. In spite of the cold reception she had received from Dolores Webster and the chilling voice on the tape, she was happy that she had made it to the house and felt a sense of relief.

Janis opened the drawer where she had placed the cassette player and lifted it out. Turning down the volume, she replayed the ominous message and tried to determine whether the voice belonged to a man or a woman. But it had been deliberately disguised, so there was no way she could know even that much.

Why wasn't she welcome at Winter House? Janis could think of no one who did not want her there. No one but Floyd Phillips. And Janis knew that he certainly couldn't have placed the tape player in her room. Floyd was back in New York. Or was he?

There was a light, quick rap on the door and Janis was jolted out of her reverie. She pivoted and hesitated a moment before she opened it. Perhaps it was the person who had left the strange cassette in her room.

Resolutely, Janis flung open the door. A tall, scarecrow-thin man of about fifty, dressed in a faded cotton shirt and dust-covered Levi's, stood there.

"You Miss Long?" he asked in a guttural voice.

Janis was so taken aback that she merely nodded.

"I'm Jonas, the gardener. Got your things here. Where do you want 'em?"

Janis stood aside and said, "Pleased to meet you, Jonas. Just bring them inside. Anywhere is fine."

Jonas stared at Janis for a moment. His eyes were a light blue, and somehow they sent an involuntarily chill down Janis's spine. But she tried not to show her uneasiness. Jonas picked up Janis's luggage and brought it into the room. Even though he was tall and thin, Janis got the impression that Jonas was a very strong person.

"Sorry to have inconvenienced you," Janis said, but she could not make the words convey any warmth.

Jonas just shrugged as he gave her the car keys. "That's what I get paid for. No inconvenience to me."

After he was gone, Janis quickly forgot about Jonas and his unfriendly ways. She unpacked her things and then took a warm, leisurely bath. When she had dressed again, she felt relaxed and surprisingly alert. She wandered about the room for a while, looking for something to read, but there was nothing. Since this was the home of Clifford Green, the publisher, Janis knew that he just had to have a library. It was downstairs, no doubt.

Leaving the lamp burning on a small table by the canopied bed, Janis walked out of her room and into the dimly lit corridor. The second floor was quiet, yet

Janis had the strange sensation that she was being watched as she walked to the head of the staircase. She tried in vain to dismiss this fear, telling herself she was only imagining it.

Despite these distracting thoughts, Janis could not help noticing the antique furniture that graced the second-floor corridor. Although she was not too educated along those lines, she did see that the pieces seemed to be extremely old and extremely expensive. The perfect background for Elyse's adventures.

As Janis started to descend the staircase, a door behind her opened and she turned to face a man who made her gasp in astonishment.

"Did I startle you?" the man said, and there was a faintly amused smile on his lips.

"In a way. It's just that you bear such a striking resemblance to your father," Janis said, feeling somewhat awkward.

"Well, of course, I resemble my father. I'm Lucas Green, a chip off the old block," he said, and there was a trace of sarcasm in his voice.

"I'm Janis Long. Please forgive me for staring," she said.

A brief smile flashed across Lucas's rather thin lips. In his way, he was quite handsome. Lucas was taller than his father and more muscular. Still, their builds were similar. It was his eyes that made the difference between him and his father.

The mischievous twinkle that always seemed to be present in the publisher's eyes was missing from his son's. Lucas seemed to be staring at Janis with an intensity that made her want to avoid his eyes. But she told herself she would not be intimidated by Lucas, and she met his stare with unblinking eyes.

"I know," Lucas said. "Dad said that you would be coming. He said you would have the run of the house and that you were not to be interrupted in your work."

"Clifford Green can be a terrible taskmaster," Janis said in an attempt at levity.

Lucas said, "Yes, Dad is quite a determined man. Anyway, welcome to Winter House, Miss Long. How long do you plan on staying?"

The question was an ill-chosen one, Janis thought, considering the fact that she had just arrived a short time before.

But she did not want to antagonize Clifford's son, so she shrugged and said, "As long as it takes to complete the illustrations for the new Elyse book. I don't want to be a bother."

Lucas Green shrugged this time. "You aren't any bother. Winter House is a big place. Big enough to accommodate quite a few people."

"Yes, I can see that," Janis said. "I was on my way to find something to read. Would you mind telling me where I might find the library?"

"You'll find the library opposite the dining room," Lucas said. And when he saw the puzzled look on Janis's face, he added, "It's the second door on your left on the ground floor."

Janis thanked him and continued to walk down the staircase, feeling Lucas's eyes on her. He was neither friendly nor unfriendly. She really did not quite know how to take Clifford Green's son. However, she did not want to make any hasty decisions in regard to him. They had just met. Maybe in time she would get to know Clifford Green's son better.

The door to the library was open and Janis walked inside. Two entire walls contained shelves of books, which came as no surprise to Janis. On the mahogany desk she saw a copy of the last Elyse book, and a faint smile tugged at her lips. She had a feeling that Winnifred had been in the room and had left the book in such a conspicuous place. Just seeing the book and her name on the jacket made her feel good.

After looking at the shelves for a while, Janis chose a book of short stories by a current celebrated author. She was about to turn when a voice came from behind her.

"I see you not only illustrate books, but you read them too," said Tim Roark.

Turning, Janis stared at the handsome six-footer who was standing in the doorway.

"You do get around, don't you?" Janis said in a sharp tone of voice that revealed her irritation.

"Like I told you, I'm a frequent visitor at Winter House," Tim said, and an easy smile appeared on his full, sensuous lips.

"I seem to recall you saying something to that effect," was Janis's reply.

"Actually, I wanted to be certain that you made it to the house safe and sound."

"You didn't have to come all the way over here for that. You did follow me. And there are telephones, you know."

Instead of anger at that remark, Tim laughed. It was a deep, infectious laugh that brought a smile to Janis's lips. It was difficult not to like Tim Roark and he seemed fully aware of his charm.

"Now that's better," he said. "I was beginning to

think that you were incapable of smiling."

"It all depends on the humor," Janis replied, trying not to be taken in by Tim Roark's undeniable charm.

"You'll be a welcome addition to this house," Tim said. "Everyone will like you."

"I'm not so sure about that," Janis said.

The smile temporarily left Tim's face. "What do you mean?"

Not knowing why she should confide in a perfect stranger, Janis told Tim about finding the tape cassette and the message that both she and Mary Lee heard upstairs in her bedroom. Tim listened intently, slowly raising one curious eyebrow as Janis concluded her story.

"You aren't going to take that tape seriously, are you?"

"Why not?" she asked.

Again Tim flashed his easy smile. "It sounds to me as though someone was having a joke at your expense."

"That's what I first thought."

"Now you don't?"

Janis sighed deeply. "I don't know what to think. Maybe if I hadn't been traveling all day, I might look at it differently. But maybe you're right. It must be somebody's idea of a practical joke."

"I would hate to think that you've gotten a bad first impression of Call's Bay."

"Who's gotten a bad impression of Call's Bay?" Dolores Webster said as she stepped into the room from the hallway.

Somehow Janis got the impression that Dolores had been in the corridor for some time. She wondered just how much the cool, statuesque beauty had overheard.

"Dolores, have you met Janis Long?" Tim said, and Dolores sidled close to him as her hazel eyes narrowed just a fraction.

"Yes, we've met. But I didn't think you knew our houseguest."

"Only met her recently," Tim said as he shifted his gaze from Janis to Dolores.

Dolores immediately changed her rather chilling expression to one of practiced warmth and took hold of Tim's arm.

"It was nice of you to drop by, Tim. I really hadn't expected to see you tonight."

"Actually, I came by to see that Janis was settled in. And to borrow a book from the library. When she stopped by my place earlier, she appeared to be lost and somewhat confused."

Dolores shot Janis a sudden, angry look, but when she spoke, there was no hostility in her voice. "As you can see, our Janis is just fine. But I did want to discuss something with you, Tim. Would you excuse us please, Janis?"

Before Janis could reply, Dolores had walked out of the room, taking a somewhat reluctant Tim Roark with her. After they had gone, Janis stood there for a moment or two, staring at the wall across the corridor. It was very apparent that Dolores had staked her claim on Tim Roark. And it was also very clear that she did not want any interference from Janis Long.

With a slight shrug, Janis turned and walked over to one of the antique chairs. It could have been a Queen Anne, but she was not certain. At the moment, she was more interested in what had just taken place than she was in the furniture. It did not take any great stretch of her imagination to understand that Tim Roark had the run of the house.

He had obviously entered the house on his own. And he'd mentioned that he had a key. She idly wondered if he could have been the one who had left the cassette tape in her bedroom. After all, he had not seemed particularly pleased when she had stopped at his house for help. And he did know all about her.

But why would Tim Roark not want her to remain at Winter House? Or why would anybody else resent her presence, for that matter? She would just have to stop thinking about the tape or she would become paranoid about it.

Sitting down in the library, Janis began to scan the pages of the book. After a while she found herself engrossed in one of the stories. By the time she had finished reading it, she was quite sleepy.

Closing the book, she got to her feet, turned out the library light, and headed for the stairs. Janis was so tired that she felt as though she were walking in her sleep. The strange, unfamiliar house only added to her weariness.

As she started to walk up the stairs, the lights flickered for a moment. At first Janis thought it was just her imagination, but as she continued to mount the stairs, they went out altogether.

For a moment, Janis just stood there, and then panic began to sweep over her and she moved to the right and grabbed the railing. Just as she did so, she felt someone push past her. If she had not moved when she did, she would have been hurled down the staircase.

CHAPTER FOUR

"Who's there?" Janis called out in the darkness that surrounded her.

There was no answer. Whoever had tried to push her down the staircase was no longer around. Using the railing on the staircase, Janis continued to climb the stairs, and the lights came on again.

"Janis! Are you all right?" called a voice from the bottom of the stairs. It was Mary Lee and her eyes were wide with concern.

"Yes, I'm fine. But I had a close call up here."

"A close call? What do you mean?" Dolores Webster said as she and Tim Roark appeared at the foot of the stairs next to Mary Lee.

Janis quickly decided that she would not tell Tim Roark what had happened on the staircase. At least not in front of Dolores. She had already gone too far by telling Tim about the cassette tape she had found in her room earlier that night.

"It was nothing," Janis said as Lucas Green ambled out of the library and came to stand behind Dolores and Tim. "I guess I just got a little skittery about being plunged into the dark. My imagination was working overtime."

"I know what you mean," Dolores said. "Tim had left me alone. You shouldn't have done that, Tim. Anything might have happened to me in the dark."

Dolores was using all her feminine wiles on Tim and that bothered Janis.

But then she thought, Tim has known Dolores far longer than he has me.

That didn't make her feel much better.

Tim had left Dolores's side and was walking up the stairs toward Janis. Looking down, Janis could see the hateful look in Dolores's eyes.

"You don't look so good," Tim said as he reached Janis. "As a matter of fact, you're trembling. Are you sure you're all right?"

"As I said, I'm perfectly all right," Janis said with a slight tremble.

"No, you're not," Tim said, taking one of her arms. "I'm going to take you into the kitchen for a cup of warm milk."

Before Janis could protest, Tim had led her down the stairs.

As they passed Dolores, the brunette said, "That's a good idea, Tim. Would you see me in the library before you leave?"

Tim didn't answer and Janis heard Dolores turn and walk briskly away. When Janis and Tim passed Lucas,

Janis glanced at Lucas's face, but it was a mask that she could not fathom.

Mary Lee was alongside of her as she was being led toward the kitchen. "That's the first time we've ever had an electric failure here. Honestly, Miss Long, that's the truth."

"I'm Janis, remember?" Janis said, managing a weak smile for the friendly girl.

Mary Lee returned the smile as she opened the kitchen door. Then she took some milk from the refrigerator.

"Would it be too much trouble if I fixed myself a cup of hot chocolate?" Janis said. "Just tell me where everything is, Mary Lee. I'll make it myself. You must be getting tired. I don't want to make you wait on me."

Instead of looking offended, Mary Lee gave a sigh of relief. "I am kind of tired. Mother and I have rooms off the kitchen. Jonas sleeps on the third floor. And the cocoa, by the way, is on the second shelf."

With that Mary Lee said good night and left Janis and Tim alone. Janis offered to make Tim some hot chocolate, but he decided to have some coffee. There was an electric percolator plugged into the wall. He poured himself a cup and took a seat at the table.

While Janis fixed her hot chocolate, Tim said, "You sure that you're all right? You're just not saying that for my benefit?"

Janis glanced at Tim, who was taking a sip from his cup of coffee. She wondered just how serious he really was and if he really did care how she was feeling. It was just possible that he might have been the person who had left the cassette in her room and he also could have been the one who had rushed past her on the stairs. Until she really got to know him better, she felt she should not confide in him.

"Thanks for your concern, but I'm really fine now. It was just being in the dark in a strange house that got to me for a minute there. You must think that I'm a real ninny."

Tim shook his head. "I haven't come to any conclusions as far as you're concerned. Although you did look pretty pathetic standing there all alone on the staircase."

Janis poured the hot chocolate into a mug and walked over to the table. She took a seat before she spoke.

"Believe me, after living in New York, I'm not easily frightened."

"This all must seem pretty rustic to you after the big city," Tim said, glancing at her with his dark eyes.

"Believe it or not, I don't miss New York that much. I actually am looking forward to staying in Oregon for a while. And Clifford Green has been very kind to me. When a book editor showed him my work, he backed me all the way. If it wasn't for him, I wouldn't be an illustrator or staying here at Winter House."

Tim said, "You and Clifford are good friends, I take it."

"Just friends," Janis said, and she noticed that a slight smile tugged at Tim's lips. "He thought I could use Winter House as background material for the new Elyse book. And from what I've seen of the house, he made a good choice."

"You are referring, I take it, to all the antiques that are in the place," Tim said, then took a sip from his cup.

"I'm not a connoisseur, but from what I've seen, there are some priceless things here," Janis said. "If the place belonged to me, I would be worried about all those fine old pieces."

"I think all of Clifford's antiques are safe out here in the wilds of Oregon," Tim said. "The house is isolated and there aren't that many people who know about Winter House and its treasures."

"You're probably right," Janis said with a sigh. "Maybe I was just overreacting. Incidentally, since you know all about me, Tim Roark, why not tell me about you?"

Tim looked at Janis from beneath his dark eyebrows. "What do you want to know? And why?"

"I guess it's just my interest in people. When I meet someone new, I like to find out as much as I can about him or her."

"For future reference?" Tim said in an amused tone of voice. "Do you plan on using me as an illustration in one of your future books?"

"It's possible," Janis said, and she couldn't help but smile at Tim, who could be quite personable when he tried.

"In that case, I'm single, unattached. I've lived here in Oregon off and on for about five years. I'm an architect by trade, but I'm independently wealthy, thanks to the wise planning of my father and mother, both of whom are deceased."

It was all said so mechanically that Janis got the impression Tim had made that speech many times in the past.

"You said that you live here off and on? What does that mean?"

Tim shrugged his wide shoulders. "In my line of work, I travel a great deal. My place here in Oregon is as near to a home as I've had in years."

"You must like your place here. Apparently, you keep coming back to Oregon."

"The house is all right. Not what I have in mind as a permanent residence."

"Someday I'd like to hear what your idea of a permanent residence might be," Janis said.

Tim smiled at that. "Okay, I've filled you in on my life. Turnabout's fair play. What about you, Janis Long? So far all I know about you is that you're an illustrator. That you come from New York and that you know Clifford Green."

Janis was about to speak when the door to the kitchen opened and Lucas Green walked in.

He glanced quickly at the two of them and said, "Dolores is asking for you, Tim. But I see that you're pretty well occupied."

A faint look of annoyance flashed across Tim's face, but it was gone as quickly as it had appeared. Tim's smile seemed forced as he said, "I'll be right there. Was there anything else?"

Lucas shook his head and walked out of the kitchen. Janis couldn't help but notice that Lucas and Tim were not exactly fond of each other.

"Now that I know that you're all right, I'd better get back to Dolores," Tim said as he got to his feet. He walked to the door and then paused, as though he had just thought of something. "You aren't married or anything?"

Janis was taken aback by what Tim had said, but she quickly recovered. "At the moment, no," she said, and then Tim walked out of the kitchen.

Janis sat there for a while, finishing her hot chocolate. She could hear the sighing of the wind outside the kitchen window. It was a lonely, mournful sound. Suddenly, she felt exhausted. The hot chocolate was certainly doing its work on her.

Janis got to her feet and rinsed her cup, leaving it on the counter. She glanced out the kitchen window and thought she saw the movement of someone in the dense growth of trees beyond the house. Janis strained her eyes to see more clearly. But there was nobody out there. Suddenly, for no explainable reason, she thought about Floyd Phillips. Had he really, after all, followed her from New York? Perhaps it had been Floyd that she had seen at the motel last night. Could he have now begun stalking her here at Winter House? The very thought sent a ripple of fear down Janis's spine.

She turned and walked out of the kitchen and into the dim, shadowy corridor. From the library she could hear the low hum of voices. Tim and Dolores's voices. The thought of Tim being with Dolores gave Janis a queasy feeling in her stomach. Or was it just the hot chocolate?

Shaking off the memory of what had happened on the stairs earlier, Janis walked wearily up to the second floor. Here it was quiet, too quiet. She glanced nervously around as she headed toward her room.

As she opened her door, Janis paused for a moment just in case there was someone inside. She peered around cautiously and then, assured that the room was empty, she walked in. It was just as she had left it. Nothing had been disturbed.

"Why did you think that anything would be disturbed?" she muttered to herself. "This isn't some mystery novel."

But Janis had to admit that Winter House was the perfect setting for a mystery story. Especially tonight with the wind howling and the rain beating against the window. It was a light rain, but the wind thrashed it against the panes with vehemence.

By the time Janis had gotten ready for bed, the rain and the wind had both ceased. She glanced out of the closed window and saw a sprinkling of stars through a break in the clouds. The room was suddenly stuffy. Janis decided that she would open the window just a trifle so that she could enjoy the cool night air.

Then she slipped between the crisp sheets and sighed. Even though she had earlier been overwhelmed with drowsiness, she suddenly felt wide awake. She wished that she had brought that book up with her, but she must have dropped it on the stairs. She reached out and turned off the lamp on the nightstand.

Forcing herself to relax, Janis finally felt her eyelids grow heavy, and she drifted off into a deep sleep. At first her dream was pleasant. She was with her parents in their cozy home. Then suddenly her dream changed. She found herself in Winter House. Only, it wasn't the real Winter House. This house was made of glass and she was all alone. For some reason, Janis suddenly felt panicky. Something or someone was threatening her. Then she saw Floyd Phillips. He was standing at the top of the staircase.

"You'll never get away from me," he shouted at her.

Janis began to run, to try and find a way out of the house. But there were no doors in the house. She was trapped inside this house of glass. She turned and saw Floyd slowly descending the staircase. That only prompted her to try even harder to get out of the house.

She beat her fists against the glass, trying desperately to break it. Behind her she could hear the footsteps of Floyd Phillips as he drew nearer. Then she felt a hand touch her shoulder, and she was slowly forced to turn around.

Janis awoke with a start. She sat up in bed, confused by the darkness and the unfamiliar surroundings. She reached out and flicked on the light. A sudden chill touched her shoulders, and she turned to see the curtains at the window billowing in a breeze.

Getting out of bed, Janis padded across the carpet to the window and reached out to close it. She paused in mid-action. There was something wrong with the window, she thought. She couldn't remember having opened it that far. She was certain that she had only opened it a fraction.

Janis shivered as she closed the window. Then as her eyes lowered, she noticed damp spots on the rug. Not from the rain, she thought. These were from somebody's shoes. Janis stared in disbelief at what she saw. Somebody had been in her room while she slept.

CHAPTER FIVE

Janis did not know how long she stood there, staring at the rug, but after a while she got back in bed, switched off the light, and pulled the covers up to her chin. It gave her an eerie feeling to know that someone had been in her room. Who had it been and what did he or she want?

After tossing and turning for a half hour, she managed to get back to sleep. Janis's dreams were uneasy and full of phantoms.

When she awoke, it was morning and the bright sunlight streaming into her room almost made her forget about the nightmares of the previous night.

After she had taken a quick, bracing shower, she dressed in a pair of dark slacks and a tangerine sweater. She brushed her blond hair until it fairly crackled, then walked over to the window. By now the footprints had

38

faded away. There was no proof that anyone had been in her room last night. But Janis knew that she hadn't been dreaming that someone had opened the window and entered her room. Just why was something that she aimed to find out.

The corridor was empty as Janis walked to the stairs, but she still had the uneasy feeling that eyes were following her.

When she got to the bottom of the stairs, Winnifred met her.

"Good morning, Miss Long," the housekeeper said with a wide smile on her face.

"Janis, please."

"Very well, Janis. Did you sleep well?"

"I wasn't used to the strange room and a new bed. You know how that goes," Janis said, not wanting to tell Winnifred the real reason she hadn't gotten a good night's rest.

"Indeed I do. I hope you get used to the room. Breakfast is in the dining room. It's very informal. Everything's on the sideboard. Just help yourself."

"Thank you, Winnifred," Janis said as she headed toward the dining room.

Walking into the dining room, she saw that Dolores and Lucas were already seated at the vast mahogany table. The aroma of freshly brewed coffee tantalized her.

"Good morning, Miss Long," Lucas said as he raised a cup of coffee to his lips. "Just help yourself. Breakfast is pretty casual here at Winter House."

Janis acknowledged Lucas's greeting and then spoke to Dolores, who merely nodded as she munched on a buttered piece of toast.

Janis walked over to the sideboard and took a plate. She ladled some scrambled eggs and some sauted chicken livers onto her plate and filled a cup with hot, steaming coffee. Then she took a seat opposite Lucas and Dolores.

"Sleep well?" Lucas said as he took a bite of scrambled eggs.

"To a degree," Janis answered, studying the faces of the two sitting opposite her. "It must have been the strange, unfamiliar room, but at one point I got the weirdest feeling that I was not alone there last night."

Neither Lucas nor Dolores displayed any alarm.

Dolores glanced up from her food and said, "Don't tell me that Winter House has a ghost?"

"Hardly," Janis said in a level tone of voice. "I stopped believing in such things years ago. No, whoever was in my room was very much flesh and blood. As a matter of fact, my window was opened and I found fresh, damp footprints on the carpet."

Lucas stared at Janis. There was great concern on his face. "You are serious. You think there really was someone in your room. Are the footprints still there?"

Janis sighed. "They were gone this morning when I woke up. The water had dried."

"Then you might just have been dreaming," Dolores said. "But then you are an artist and you probably do have a vivid imagination."

Janis could see the mockery on Dolores's face and she tried to hide her irritation. "I can separate my artistic nature from my more practical self. But I will admit that being an artist has made me more aware of details and given me the ability to pay attention to what other people might miss or take for granted."

Lucas leaned forward. "That's very interesting. I never thought about that before. I mean, about artists seeing details that other people miss. I guess that's why my father likes your work. Because your illustrations are lifelike."

"This is all beyond me," Dolores said. "As far as children's books are concerned, I really can't classify them or their illustrations as works of art."

It was obvious that Dolores was doing her very best to get an argument from Janis. The woman had a way of rankling Janis, but Janis was determined not to let Dolores get the better of her.

"There are some excellent artists working in the children's field. However, art is a matter of personal taste," Janis said.

"I suppose," Dolores said.

"How much of Winter House do you intend to use for background on your new book?" Lucas asked, obviously wishing to change the subject.

"All of it," Janis said, and then she amended that. "At least as much of it as I can. I thought I would wander around after breakfast and get the feel of the house. See what areas of the place could be used in the new book."

"Would you like me to show you around?" Lucas asked without any real enthusiasm.

"No, thanks," Janis replied. "I work better alone."

"Not from what I saw last night," Dolores said.

"What do you mean?"

"You and Tim were being quite cozy on the stairs and in the kitchen," Dolores said, not trying to disguise her feelings. "Is Tim Roark part of your research?"

"That's ridiculous," Janis said. "Tim was just being thoughtful."

"I know," Dolores said with a wry smile on her lips. "That's part of his charm."

Before Janis could say anything further, Dolores excused herself and walked out of the room.

There was an awkward silence at the table for a few minutes and then Lucas said, "Don't mind Dolores. She's a spoiled brat. Comes from a wealthy Long Island family. Her father and my dad were close friends. When Dolores's father died, my dad took over as a surrogate father. Sometimes I think he likes Dolores better than he does me."

There was a tinge of bitterness in Lucas's words and Janis couldn't help but notice the sudden narrowing of his eyes at the mention of his father.

Then a quick, engaging smile crossed Lucas's lips. "That almost sounds like sibling rivalry, doesn't it?"

"I'm sure your father loves you very much," Janis said.

"My offer still holds to show you around," Lucas said as he put his cup down on the saucer.

"Really, I would much prefer to be on my own," Janis said.

Lucas shrugged. "Suit yourself. Only, don't get lost."

After that, they just made small talk for a few minutes. Janis got the impression that Lucas was only being polite, that he had other things to do and he was being patient with her.

"Why don't you run along?" Janis finally said. "I'm sure you have work to do."

"That's true. I have important work to do," Lucas said and got to his feet. "Enjoy yourself."

"I will."

With that remark from Janis, Lucas left the room. After he had gone, Janis sat there for a few minutes, trying to eat her breakfast. Since she had spoken to Dolores, her appetite had left her. She moved the food around on her plate for a few moments and then gave up.

She could only get down a slice of toast and that was dry and almost stuck to the roof of her mouth. She took a sip of coffee and her thoughts went back to last night, or early this morning, when she had discovered that someone had been in her room.

Dolores had made light of the fact, but Janis knew that she had not been mistaken. She had seen the damp imprints on the carpet. And the window had been raised fairly high.

But who could it have been? The first person that entered her thoughts was Floyd Phillips. Janis was beginning to be convinced that he had followed her all the way across the country and was now hiding somewhere outside Winter House. Just the thought of Floyd skulking around sent a quick chill down her spine.

If it hadn't been Floyd, then who could it have been? What motive would Tim Roark have in wanting to search her room? When she had first met him, he was surly and cynical. Then he had changed. Was all his friendliness and concern just a front? Could she trust him?

Then there was Dolores. It seemed preposterous to think that she could have managed to scale the wall outside her window and come into her room. But Dolores had a strong, determined quality about her that couldn't be overlooked.

As for Lucas, he was young and strong. And he was quite capable of scaling the wall outside her room. For whatever purpose Janis did not know. And she certainly couldn't discount Jonas, the gardener. He had been anything but friendly when he had brought her luggage up last night. But what might he want in her room? Then Janis remembered the tape recorder and the cassette tape that had been left so obviously on the chest of drawers.

Thinking of that, Janis hurried from the dining room and up the stairs to her bedroom. She opened the drawer where she had placed the tape recorder and found that it was no longer there. Somehow she was not surprised that it was gone. So that was the reason someone had entered her room, to get rid of the evidence. Janis slowly closed the drawer and left the room.

She walked idly down the corridor and tried to concentrate on all the works of art, the finely crafted furniture, but her mind was not on what she was doing. The reason she had left New York was to be rid of the uneasy feelings she was experiencing from Floyd Phillips. But here she was clear across the country and the sense of danger was once again beginning to haunt her.

Janis walked aimlessly down the staircase and through the rooms on the first floor. She had to force herself to concentrate on what she was doing. After all, Clifford Green would expect her to make good use of Winter House for her illustrations. Thinking of the text of the next Elyse book did help, and for a moment or two Janis did get some useful ideas that might be incorporated into the new book. She was in the family room when Mary Lee poked her head around the doorjamb.

"You're wanted on the telephone, Janis. Long distance."

"Long distance? Who is it?" Janis said, for a moment fearful that something had happened to her parents.

"Clifford Green," Mary Lee said and was gone.

Janis had seen the telephone in the library and she hurried down the hallway to speak with Clifford Green. He was very cheerful, and the sound of his strong voice was very reassuring to Janis.

"I'm glad you arrived safe and sound. What do you think of Winter House? Is it all that I told you it would be?"

Janis was quick to tell Clifford that she had a good trip, that she hadn't had time to look at the house closely, but she thought it would be perfect for the Elyse book.

"Good. I had a feeling that you would find it to your liking. Now I have some instructions for you. As long as you are living at Winter House, you are to have full rein of the place. Everything is at your disposal. I don't want anyone interfering with your work. As a matter of fact, I'm putting you in charge of the house. Do I make myself clear?"

This was rather startling news, but Janis knew better than to go against Clifford Green's wishes. When he made up his mind, that was that.

"If there is anything you need, just ask for it," Clifford said. "Now, please put that son of mine on so that

I can relay this information to him. The best of luck to you, Janis. Take your time with the book. There is no deadline."

Janis put the telephone receiver aside and walked out of the room. She could hear Lucas's voice coming from the study, which was the room next to the library. She paused before the open study door. Inside she saw Dolores and Lucas. Lucas turned from Dolores and his eyebrows rose when he saw Janis.

"You are wanted on the telephone, Lucas. It's your father," Janis said and then walked away.

She did not feel in the mood to talk to Dolores. Instead, she walked to the front door of the house. A breath of fresh air would do her good.

Outside, the sun was shining from an unclouded sky. The newly washed grass and the shrubs looked clean and smelled fresh and tantalizing. Janis was in the mood for a long walk.

Taking a pathway that led away from the house, Janis ambled along, taking in the breathtaking beauty that surrounded her. This was such a far cry from New York that she wanted to savor every minute of it.

The trail wound its way through some pine trees to the cliff overlooking the ocean. Standing on the promontory, Janis could see the angry sea below her as it dashed against the glistening rocks in the cove. It was an awesome sight and Janis stood there almost in a trance, watching the restless movement of the water.

Suddenly, she felt a coolness behind her as a shadow temporarily blocked the rays of the sun. A quick chill went down her body. Somebody was standing directly behind her.

The first name that flashed through her mind was

Floyd Phillips. He had finally found her! Then a hand reached out and touched her shoulder. The movement was so unexpected that Janis shrieked.

CHAPTER SIX

"Am I that frightening?" a familiar voice asked.

Janis pivoted to see Tim Roark standing behind her. There was an amused smile on his face.

"You startled me," Janis said, feeling the color rise in her cheeks. She hated it when her embarrassment showed in this obvious way, a carry-over from her childhood.

"Sorry, I thought you heard me. Believe me, I don't go around frightening people. Am I forgiven?"

Gazing into Tim's face and seeing a genuine look of regret, Janis couldn't be angry with him.

"Of course. I guess I'm still not used to all this space. I hope I don't spend the rest of my time here at Winter House jumping at shadows."

"You'll get used to it. Part of the charm of Winter House is its isolation. And this beautiful view. It should be an inspiration to you as an artist."

"It's lovely. Such atmosphere! A little intimidating but nonetheless lovely. I'll have to do some sketches of it before I leave."

"It's a little early to be speaking of leaving. You just more or less arrived," Tim said in a teasing tone of voice.

"I never know how long it will take me to do an Elyse book. I could be out of here within a week or maybe a month or longer."

Tim appeared to be very interested in how long she would remain at Winter House. "Let's hope that you find it takes you a while to do this book."

"I didn't know that you were interested in children's books," Janis couldn't help saying.

"I have a variety of interests," Tim said, smiling. "Even Winter House interests me."

Janis was about to ask him in what way when Tim abruptly said, "Speaking of atmosphere, how would you like to see our rain forest?"

"A rain forest? Just what is that?"

"Something that time forgot. Giant ferns, towering trees, and ferocious animals."

"Ferocious animals?" Janis said. "I don't think I'd like that very much."

"These animals are ferocious in appearance only. They're just replicas from the age of dinosaurs. No tourist should come to Winter House without seeing the rain forest."

Janis considered the rain forest for a moment or two. Tim made it sound very interesting. What did she have to lose? Who knew? Maybe she might somehow be able to work this rain forest into the book illustrations.

"Well, I don't want to be an exception to that rule," Janis said.

Tim's smile broadened. "Does that mean that you would like to go?"

"Very much so," Janis said, amused at Tim's little-boy attitude.

"Good. How about tomorrow? It just so happens that I have a free day. I'll pick you up. Shall we say about nine o'clock?"

"Nine o'clock would be fine," Janis said, hardly able to keep the excitement out of her voice.

"I knew I could count on you. You appeared to me to be the adventurous type," Tim said.

"Not really. But I do enjoy seeing different places and things. I was so busy driving across country that I really couldn't enjoy enough of the scenery. It's good to be able to follow a more relaxed routine."

"Routine?" One eyebrow rose inquisitively on Tim's handsome face.

"Oh, we artists are disciplined, you know," Janis said in an exaggerated tone of voice, and Tim immediately understood her humor. "We just couldn't get any work done otherwise. But then you know all about that being an architect."

"Fortunately, I am now able to work only when a job appeals to me," Tim said. "However, that doesn't mean that I'm lazy. Far from it. My parents instilled a pride in working in me when I was just a small child."

Janis listened intently as Tim spoke. This was another side of the handsome architect that she hadn't been aware of. Even though he obviously was quite well-to-do, he was not one of the snobbish rich. He apparently enjoyed working.

"You are lucky, aren't you?" Janis said. "I like working and being creative. Even though I'm not financially independent I make my own way in the world."

"Commendable," Tim said.

Janis searched his face for any sign of mockery, but Tim obviously had meant what he had said.

After that they chatted for a few minutes and then Janis decided that she had better get back to the house. "After all, I am a working girl and it's time to start acting like one."

She left Tim standing at the edge of the cliff as she walked back to Winter House. Once she glanced over her shoulder and she saw Tim watching her. Janis experienced a strange feeling in the pit of her stomach. In all her life she had never met a man quite like Tim Roark, never known anyone who affected her the way he did. Janis was not certain what to make of this feeling. Could she actually be falling in love with him? That seemed highly unlikely since she had just barely met the man. Yet there was certainly something special about him.

"You'd better get to work, Janis, my girl," she murmured to herself as she quickened her steps.

Winter House now seemed silent except for Mary Lee, who waved at Janis as she carried an armload of linen up the staircase. Of all the people Janis had met since coming to the house, Mary Lee was the most open and honest. Possibly Winnifred was the same too. A case of daughter taking after her mother.

Janis wandered about the huge house, this time really concentrating on the furnishings and the paintings and the other art objects. Now that she was giving the place her full attention, she saw how priceless most of the furnishings were in Winter House. Clifford Green certainly had invested a great deal of money in the house.

Pausing in the study, Janis found herself looking at two chairs that stood side by side. They were alike in every detail except for the bears that were carved in the backs of the chairs. The animals faced each other as though they were about to engage in deadly combat. Janis involuntarily suppressed a slight shudder. Even though the chairs were a work of fine craftsmanship, she did not like them. They seemed savage. She turned and walked out of the room.

"Researching?" came the voice of Lucas Green, who was standing in the corridor.

"Yes," Janis said. "Your father certainly was one for collecting rare furniture."

A slight twist touched the edges of Lucas Green's lips. "One thing I'll say for Dad, he certainly did get around in his travels. And he has a good eye for the valuable. There is a fortune tied up in this house."

"I can very well believe that," Janis said.

"Well, I'll leave you to your research. If you need me, I'll be in the library," Lucas said in a not unpleasant tone of voice.

As he walked away, Janis wondered just what Clifford Green had told his son on the telephone. Clifford, she knew from past experience, could be quite curt when he chose to be. She very much doubted that he would treat his relatives any different than he did other people. But then Lucas knew his father's moods far better than she did.

Janis decided that she would go to her room and reread the manuscript for the new Elyse book. That way she could refresh her memory and also see how the text meshed with various parts of Winter House.

Taking the manuscript from her small briefcase, Janis kicked off her shoes and curled up on the bed. However, she found that she couldn't concentrate on the pages before her.

Instead, her thoughts were drifting back to last night and the episode on the staircase. Who had brushed against her while she was standing on the stairs? And if she hadn't moved, would she have fallen and been injured?

Janis shifted her position on the bed and then her attention was directed to the window once again. Had it been the same person on the stairs who had entered her room last night and taken away the ominous cassette tape? It all seemed so senseless.

Once again Janis tried to concentrate on the manuscript. She reached for a pencil and began to make some marginal notes, ideas that might lead to illustrations. But even as she did so, she couldn't stop the other thoughts that crept into her mind. Thoughts about Floyd Phillips and his threats. Was he at this very moment somewhere near Winter House just waiting his chance to do some harm to her?

Janis wouldn't put it past Floyd to have been the one who had scaled the wall outside her bedroom. He was just the type of person who would do such a thing.

Still, it could very well have been someone else. Tim Roark was strong enough to have made the climb and Janis still did not know him well enough to place him above suspicion. He had seemed friendly enough when she had met him on the cliff overlooking the ocean. But there was something about the handsome architect, something that he appeared to be holding back, that disturbed Janis.

Picking up the manuscript, Janis got off the bed and walked over to the desk. She now took out her sketch pad and checked her art supplies in order to keep her mind off her problems. For a while this seemed to work, but when she glanced across the room to the chest of drawers, she immediately thought about the intruder and the missing tape deck.

Since the cassette tape and the recorder had been stolen, she did not have any proof that she had been threatened. She should have been more cautious. She should have hidden the cassette player somewhere else in the room. Yet if she had, then perhaps the person who had stolen it might have inflicted bodily harm on her in order to make her tell where she had hidden the thing.

"This has got to stop," Janis said aloud. "You're beginning to sound like someone in a TV soap opera."

Hearing these words spoken aloud gave Janis the balance that had been lacking in the past few hours. Even though she was an artist, she did have a practical side. This down-to-earth quality kept her from becoming too vulnerable and easily frightened. Usually.

Janis spent most of the day in her room doing one preliminary sketch after another. She had gotten so well acquainted with the personality of Elyse that she could have drawn the little girl's face in her sleep. In some ways Elyse's facial expressions were like her own. Janis had sometimes stared into the mirror for hours making different faces at herself.

These expressions sometimes appeared in the Elyse

books. Yet Elyse had taken on a personality all her own. Janis had grown quite fond of the impetuous little child and there was even talk of an Elyse doll coming out sometime in the near future.

Dinner that evening was a somewhat somber affair. When Janis entered the dining room, she found that only Lucas was there. She felt a sense of relief that she wouldn't be subjected to the haughty glances of Dolores Webster. But that relief was short-lived. For soon Dolores walked in wearing a mauve-colored kaftan. And looking coolly beautiful.

"How was your day?" Lucas asked. "Get a lot of work done?"

"A fair amount," Janis answered. "I've begun a few sketches."

"Father gave me instructions that you are to have the run of the house," Lucas said, sounding somewhat resentful. "He made that quite clear on the telephone."

Janis said nothing. It had not been her idea to take over the place. And if Clifford Green had made his intentions clear on the telephone, there was nothing she could say about it.

"You don't intend to stay cooped up here at Winter House, do you?" Dolores said in a chilly tone of voice.

"As a matter of fact, I don't," Janis replied. "Tim Roark has asked me to go with him to see the rain forest tomorrow."

These words brought an angry look to Dolores's eyes and she gazed at Janis with unmistakable hatred.

Janis was glad when the meal was finished and she and Lucas were left in the dining room alone. Dolores had made some excuse as she left the room.

After she was gone, the conversation between Janis and Lucas drifted back to Clifford Green.

"You know, my father can be quite generous to everyone but his own family. He has reduced my monthly check considerably in the past year. But that doesn't bother me. I can get along just fine without his help. I've found a way to bring in enough money to keep me very well satisfied."

Janis was about to pursue this further when she happened to glance out the window. It was still quite light outside, and she caught a glimpse of someone standing there. It was a man. But he was quickly gone. Immediately, Janis thought about Floyd Phillips and she couldn't restrain the gasp of surprise that escaped her lips.

CHAPTER SEVEN

"What's the matter?" Lucas asked. "What did you see?"

"I saw someone at the window. A man, I think," Janis said, her voice catching in her throat. "Just caught a glimpse. Then he was gone."

Lucas looked at the window. "Are you certain?" he said. "I don't see anyone. Maybe you just imagined it."

"I didn't imagine it. There was a man standing there. I saw him against the window," Janis said.

There was still plenty of sunlight so that both she and Lucas could see outside. Lucas got slowly to his feet.

"Maybe I'd better have a look around, Janis. We don't often get prowlers around here, since Winter House is so isolated."

Janis pushed her chair back and got to her feet also.

As Lucas walked out of the room, Janis followed him.

"Did you get a good look at him?" Lucas said over his shoulder.

"No. It was very fast. And his face was in the shadows."

"Well, he couldn't have gotten very far. If there is someone out there, I'll find him."

Lucas reached for the front door and flung it open.

"Now that's what I call service," said Tim Roark, who was standing in the doorway. "I was just about to ring the doorbell."

"Roark," Lucas said, somewhat startled by the appearance of the architect. "How long have you been out there?"

"I just arrived," Tim said. "Is something wrong?"

Lucas nodded his head toward Janis. "Janis thinks she saw a man standing at a window in the dining room. I was on my way to check it out."

"Who was it, Janis?" Tim asked.

"Just a man. I didn't get a good look at his face," Janis said, a little nervous under the close scrutiny of Tim Roark's unblinking eyes.

"Maybe you just thought you saw someone," he said. "Did you see him, Lucas?"

"No, I didn't. But Janis said he was just there for a second."

"I see," Tim said.

"Did you see anybody on the grounds when you arrived?" Lucas asked.

"Not a soul. But then I wasn't expecting to see a prowler around here."

"You're both wasting time," Janis said irritably. "He might still be out there."

"She's right," Tim said. "Come on, Lucas. Let's have a look around before it gets dark."

"I'm going with you," Janis said as she moved toward the open door.

Tim barred her way. "No, you're not. You wait here. We'll be right back."

"Dolores, you and Janis stay inside," Lucas said.

Janis turned to see Dolores standing behind them.

After Lucas and Tim had gone, Dolores said, "What's going on around here? Where are Tim and Lucas going?"

"They're looking for someone," Janis said.

"Who?"

"Someone I saw looking in the window in the dining room," Janis said, and she saw Dolores raise a skeptical eyebrow.

"Seeing people now?" Dolores said in a caustic tone of voice.

"Whether you believe it or not, I did," Janis said emphatically. "He was standing at the window, watching Lucas and me."

"Let's go in the study. I'll ask Mary Lee to bring us some coffee, and you can tell me all about this mysterious man you saw."

Janis could hardly contain her anger as she walked toward the study. She knew that Dolores did not like her and wouldn't believe anything she had to say. She knew that as long as she remained at Winter House the two of them just would not get along.

Walking into the study, Janis went to the window and peered out. There was still quite a bit of daylight left and she gazed at the trees that bordered the house. Perhaps somewhere out there was the man she had seen. Could it possibly be Floyd Phillips? Was he trying to frighten her into leaving Winter House and returning to New York where he intended to pick up on their relationship?

Or maybe it wasn't Floyd at all. Tim Roark had certainly made an unexpected and timely appearance. It was possible that Tim had been the one she had seen. But Janis did not want to think it was Tim. She had grown too fond of him. But was that wise?

"Come away from that window." Dolores's voice came from behind her, and Janis involuntarily turned to face the beautiful but disagreeable woman.

"Let's have a cup of coffee. Winnifred always has some ready," Dolores said as she placed a tray on a coffee table. "All of this nonsense is beginning to get to me."

"It isn't nonsense," Janis said as she walked over to where Dolores stood. "Even though Lucas didn't see anyone, I most certainly did."

Dolores shrugged and sat down. "Maybe it was that weird gardener. He's just the type who would be staring in through windows. Frankly, the man gives me the creeps. I don't know why Clifford puts up with him."

Janis hadn't thought of Jonas. Maybe Dolores was right. It could have been the gardener. Janis felt a sense of relief at that thought. If it had been Jonas, then it couldn't have been Floyd Phillips. He was probably back in New York. Maybe he might even have found himself another girl.

"Then you do believe that I saw someone," Janis said, pouring herself a cup of coffee.

"I never said I didn't." Dolores took a sip from her cup.

"Somehow I got the idea that you didn't believe me," Janis said.

"You do have an active imagination," Dolores said. "That episode on the stairs last night, for one thing. You'd better watch yourself, Miss Long. You'll be hearing voices next."

Janis shot Dolores an angry look as she took a seat as far away from Dolores as she could.

"And another thing," Dolores said, "stay away from Tim Roark."

"Tim Roark? What do you mean?" Janis asked.

"You know very well what I mean. You aren't fooling me. Ever since you've arrived, you've done all you could to get his attention."

Janis was taken aback by that remark. She didn't know what to say.

"Tim and I have been good friends for quite some time," Dolores said. "I met him in Denver a few years ago and he sees me whenever we both happen to be in Oregon."

"I can assure you that I have no interest in Tim Roark," Janis said. "And if I had, I don't think that's any concern of yours. Since, as you say, you're both just friends."

Dolores's eyes narrowed into tiny, evil slits. "As I told you, stay away from him. If you know what's good for you!"

"That sounds like a threat," Janis said, not letting Dolores stare her down.

"Call it what you will," Dolores said, taking another sip of coffee.

There were voices then at the far end of the corridor. Tim and Lucas. Janis got to her feet and walked purposefully toward the study door. She saw Tim and Lucas standing nearby, their heads huddled close together. When they saw Janis, they ceased whatever conversation they were engaged in.

"Did you find whoever it was?" Janis asked them.

Tim glanced quickly at Lucas and then at Janis. There was almost a conspiratorial attitude between the two men.

"Whoever it was is gone," Tim said. "Anyway, we didn't find any traces of anyone."

"I know this may sound strange, Miss Long," Lucas said, "but are you certain that you saw somebody at the window? There wasn't anyone at the window when I looked up from the table."

"He ran away. I guess he must have known that you would look at that window after I'd seen him," Janis said, and the words somehow sounded peculiar. "Tim, you do believe me, don't you? I wouldn't make up a thing like that."

There was a slight frown on Tim's handsome face that quickly vanished as he smiled at Janis. "Of course, I believe you. Lucas and I just weren't quick enough. He had plenty of time to get away."

"That's right, Miss Long. We were just too late, I guess," Lucas said in a voice that lacked conviction.

Janis got the impression Lucas, like Dolores, did not believe her story.

"Would you two care for a cup of coffee?" Janis said in an effort to change the subject. "I know that Winnifred has some made."

"You and Tim have some," Lucas said. "I think I'll talk to Dolores. Is she in the study?"

"That's where I left her," Janis said.

Lucas paused before going into the study and cast a lingering look at Janis and Tim. Then he was gone.

"Well," Tim said, "what about that offer for a cup of coffee?"

"If you want to wait in the library, I'll bring it in," Janis said.

"The library? That sounds very formal and cold. What's wrong with the two of us sitting at that cozy table in the kitchen? We did all right there the last time," Tim said, and there was a faint, ironic twist to his full lips.

"If it's all right with Winnifred," Janis said as she headed for the kitchen.

Tim quickly caught up with her. "Are you one of those terribly efficient people? The kind that always have to have things in their proper places?"

The idea amused Janis. "Sorry, but I'm afraid you've latched onto the wrong person. My mother always listened to my dreams of becoming a great artist, and then she made me clean up the mess my room was in."

"I think I would like your mother," Tim said in a light tone of voice.

"And I'm sure she would like you," Janis said. "But then there is also my father."

"Your dad? Don't you think the two of us would hit it off?"

"This is certainly a serious turn of conversation," Janis said as she entered the kitchen. "Why all the interest in my parents?"

"Just my curious nature. When I meet someone, I want to know all about their deep, dark secrets."

"And you think I have deep, dark secrets?"

Winnifred was just finishing the dishes and said, "Miss Janis. And Tim Roark. It's always good to see you."

Tim immediately turned on all his charm. "There isn't a cook in all of Oregon that can touch you, Winnifred. When are you going to take me up on my offer and have pity on a poor, helpless bachelor?"

Winnifred wasn't about to be taken in by Tim's charm. "You, helpless! That will be the day. And, besides, I enjoy working for Clifford Green. The day I stop enjoying my work here, I just might take you up on your offer. But Mary Lee comes with me."

"I wouldn't have it any other way," Tim said. "Then you are considering my offer?"

"Only considering. What can I do for you, Miss Janis?"

"Would it be too much trouble to fix Tim and me a cup of coffee? I just had a cup with Dolores, but I could use another one."

Winnifred said it would be no trouble at all, and she quickly reached for two cups and filled them to the brim.

After she had placed them on the table before Tim and Janis, she said, "I'll leave you two alone. You probably have a lot to talk about."

Before Winnifred left, Tim said, "Don't forget my offer, Winnifred. It still stands."

"I'll think about it. Only, I have a feeling that I am going to be in Clifford Green's employ for a long time to come."

With that, Winnifred left Janis and Tim alone.

"What's all this about you asking Winnifred to come

to work for you?" Janis said after she had taken a sip of her coffee.

"It's sort of a standing joke between the two of us. I ask her to come work for me and Winnifred always refuses. Only, one day I believe I'll wear her down and she'll leave Winter House."

"That doesn't sound much like a joke to me," Janis said as she studied Tim's face.

There was a slight smile on his lips, but his eyes were not amused.

"I could, of course, just buy Winter House and get Winnifred in the bargain," Tim said.

Janis considered this for a moment or two. Was Tim really serious? Would he go to that length to get a cook for his house? From what he had told her, he did not stay in Oregon for any length of time. Such extravagance was beyond her.

They talked for about a half hour and then Tim said:

"Why don't we take a walk? You've been cooped up in this house long enough. What do you say?"

Janis couldn't think of any reason to refuse. So they walked out of the house by the kitchen door. There was a slight chill in the air, and Janis was glad that Tim took long strides so that she had to walk briskly to keep up with him. He carried most of the conversation, and Janis found that he was very knowledgeable about this part of the country, as he seemed to be about other places he had seen in his travels.

Before Janis realized it, they had come to the cliff overlooking the ocean. Below them, the angry waves beat with fury against the coastline as the sky slowly became darker around the setting sun. It was a very isolated and lonely stretch of land.

Janis looked down at the water below her that was now almost pitch black and rather frightening. She suddenly became aware that Tim had ceased talking. For some reason his silence seemed ominous.

CHAPTER EIGHT

"Are you frightened?" Tim said, as though he could read Janis's thoughts.

"Of course not," Janis said, hoping that her voice did not convey her sudden fear. "I was just thinking about the man who had been looking in the window at Lucas and me. You never found a trace of him?"

"There was nobody to find. But then he got a head start on us. I rather doubt that he would still be lingering around after you saw him. You don't have any idea who he might be?"

"I do have an idea, but right now I think I'll just wait and see what develops. This is just another incident here at Winter House."

Tim moved closer to Janis. "What do you mean by that statement? Another incident?"

"Somebody was in my room last night. Or early this morning."

"What!" Tim said and he seemed genuinely concerned. "You didn't tell me about that. Who was it?"

Janis shrugged. "I was asleep whenever he or she came in through the window. But something woke me, and when I went to close the window, I saw damp footprints on the carpet."

"I don't like the sound of this. You should have told me about this. Are the footprints still there?"

"They were gone when I checked this morning. The water dried up. So, you see, I really have no evidence. It's just my word."

"Why would anyone want to sneak into your room?" Tim asked.

"Probably to take something," Janis said. "Like the tape recorder and the tape that had been left in my room."

"Then there really was a tape in your room."

"Of course, there was," Janis said, becoming a little annoyed at Tim. "Don't tell me you didn't believe my story?"

Tim paused for a moment and then Janis heard him sigh. "To tell you the truth, I thought maybe you had made the whole thing up. Just to draw attention to yourself. After all, you do illustrate mystery stories."

"I wouldn't make a thing like that up. Besides, Mary Lee was there. She heard the tape too. You can ask her if you don't believe me."

Tim laughed. "Now don't get angry. After all, what would you have done if you'd been in my shoes? Hearing a story like that would be just a little hard to swallow. Anyway, I believe you. And I'm sorry that I didn't before."

Janis was still a trifle put out at Tim.

Then he said, "Am I forgiven?"

He said this last in such an earnest tone that Janis couldn't stay mad at him. There was no getting around the fact that Tim Roark did have winning ways and loads of charm.

"Forgiven. And I really can't say that I blame you for not believing me. I hope you don't think I'm one of those people who jump at shadows and are easily frightened."

Again Tim laughed. It was a warm, deep-throated laugh that brought a smile to Janis's face. "You, jump at shadows! That will be the day. A big-city girl like you wouldn't let something like a weird voice on a tape bother her."

Janis wasn't at all certain that Tim was right. The threatening voice had frightened her more than she cared to admit. But she wasn't about to tell that to Tim Roark. Maybe it was better if she let him think she was braver than she really was.

After all, she did not actually know Tim all that well. His could just as easily have been the disguised voice on the tape as anyone's. And he could have been behind the other things that had happened at Winter House since she had arrived.

"You know, the man at the window could have been Jonas," Tim said.

"Why do you say that?" Janis asked although Jonas was also a prime suspect in her mind.

"Who else could it have been?" Tim said. "He's the

only other man besides Lucas living at Winter House. I don't know why I didn't think of him before."

"Jonas is kind of a strange man," Janis said, not wanting to reveal how she really felt about the surly gardener.

"Never did like the man or trust him, for that matter," Tim said. "I think I'll do some checking around when I get back to the house. I'd like to know Jonas's whereabouts when you and Lucas were having dinner."

"Do you think he would tell you even if it was he that I saw?"

"It's worth a try. Maybe the element of surprise would work on him. If I just abruptly asked him, he might be caught off guard."

"The element of surprise?" came the voice of Dolores Webster, who seemed to appear from out of nowhere. "What are you talking about, Tim dear?"

Even though Janis couldn't see Dolores, she could sense how she was looking at Tim. Dolores was standing directly behind Janis, and it was all Janis could do to not turn around.

"Nothing, really. Janis and I were just having a little friendly chat," Tim said.

Dolores walked past Janis then and stood between her and Tim. "Well, I've been wanting to chat with you too, Tim. If you think you can tear yourself away from Miss Long, I have some very important matters I'd like to discuss with you."

Tim looked first at Dolores and then turned beseeching eyes on Janis, almost as though to say he was sorry that he couldn't remain with her. Janis let him off the hook.

"You two run along. I'd like to be alone for a while.

I might just wander down to the ocean. Sort of gather some more material for the book."

A sudden frown appeared on Tim's face, and he said, "Do you think you ought to do that? I mean, you should be careful where you go around here. Especially at night."

"Don't be ridiculous, Tim," Dolores said in a honey-coated voice. "Janis is a big girl. She can take care of herself."

Having said that, Dolores took Tim's arm and led him away. Janis stood there for a few moments, watching as they faded into the deepening dusk. She wondered idly just what was so important that Dolores had to speak to Tim all of a sudden.

When Tim and Janis were alone, Dolores always seemed to have an urgent problem that demanded Tim's attention. Janis tried to suppress her anger, but she couldn't. She kicked a small pebble and heard it jump down the cliff.

"Well, you're welcome to Tim Roark," Janis said aloud and then realized how childish that sounded. After all, she would be gone from Winter House in a few weeks and Tim Roark would be just a name, someone she had met while at work in Oregon.

Janis shrugged and tried to make light of her feelings for the handsome architect, but she couldn't fool herself. She found that she did care about Tim and she was upset that he was with Dolores at this very minute. But Janis couldn't blame him. In the looks department, she was sure she couldn't hold a candle to Dolores. The statuesque beauty had also known Tim far longer than Janis had and that certainly weighed the scales in Dolores's favor.

A deep sigh escaped Janis's lips as she followed a trail that apparently led down the side of the steep cliff. As she aimlessly walked, she wondered if perhaps Tim had been the one who had peered into the dining room. If he had been the one, then she would be better off alone.

The trail wound in a zigzag fashion down the cliff and Janis had to watch where she was going. She did not take her eyes off the narrow pathway. If the man at the window hadn't been Tim, then could it have been Jonas? He certainly was creepy enough to be the one.

Janis could still recall how he had looked at her when he'd brought her luggage up to her room yesterday. Yet why would Jonas be watching her? Or had he been watching her? Maybe it was Lucas that he was staring at.

Then Janis quickly dismissed this idea because she had seen the angle of the head, and the man was definitely staring at her. Yes, she realized that now.

A gust of wind suddenly swept across her, and she brushed a strand of hair out of her eyes. She could smell the seawater as she walked closer to the small stretch of beach.

Janis had reached the end of the pathway and she stood looking out across the vast ocean. Huge breakers crashed against the rocky shoals sending white spume into the air. This was a wild, untamed stretch of water and she felt small and insignificant before it.

Standing there, Janis was almost homesick for her parents in Maine and the few friends she had back in New York. Still, she did not feel that she would be glad to leave Oregon and go back East. If circumstances were different, she would actually enjoy staying at Winter House. But since Janis had arrived, there seemed to be something or someone who wanted her to leave the house.

Dolores was the first person who entered Janis's mind as she watched the angry waves rushing towards her. That woman definitely did not like her. And Janis knew the reason. It was Tim Roark. Somehow Dolores had gotten the idea that Janis was a threat to her happiness with Tim. Had Dolores been the one who had put the tape cassette in her room? That didn't seem likely since Dolores had never met Janis until she arrived at Winter House.

But maybe the brunette had heard about her from Clifford Green and had made up her mind that she was not going to like this illustrator from New York. That was a fairly plausible explanation for Dolores's cool reception. Was Dolores that insecure? It was difficult to believe that, seeing how beautiful and self-possessed the woman outwardly appeared to be.

Janis decided that it would do no good to think about Dolores. Whenever she did think of her, it was certainly not uplifting. So she began to walk casually along the shoreline, trying her best to think of anything or anyone but Dolores Webster.

As in the past, her thoughts drifted back to Floyd Phillips. Even though she had escaped from New York, she had not escaped his evil influence. He had followed her, if not physically, then emotionally. Even now, Janis couldn't be certain that it wasn't Floyd she had seen the other night at the motel.

Floyd, she well knew, was fully capable of putting the tape in her room. How he could manage that was beyond her, but Floyd had ways of gaining access to places. He had once gotten into her apartment when she had locked both her locks. Afterwards he had confessed that he had bribed the apartment manager and had told him some story about being a relative of Janis's. So if Floyd really wanted to get into Winter House, there would be no stopping him.

Janis glanced around and saw that the sun had finally settled beyond the horizon. Immediately, the shoreline and the cliff had been plunged into increasing darkness.

Janis glanced upward and saw that dark clouds obscured the moon. Only faint, blinking stars gave off any light. A quick, sickening chill crept down her spine. She never should have ventured this far from the house.

New fears soon began to invade her mind. Was it possible that whoever had been watching her at dinner was now doing the same from somewhere in that cliff?

"Stop putting those thoughts in your mind. Are you insane?" Janis murmured under her breath.

Yet she could not push aside the possibility that she was being watched. She felt it, felt the eyes of someone upon her. She immediately decided that she had to get back to the house without any further delay.

At first Janis's strides were evenly spaced, as though she wanted to give the impression that she was unaware she was being watched. It was all she could do not to bolt and run. Somehow she felt that if she acted in a normal, unhurried way, the person watching her would not make a move in her direction. She almost felt as though she were a prey for some savage beast that lay in hiding in the depths of the cliff.

She had not realized how far she had strayed from

the pathway that went up the cliff. It seemed an eternity before she finally arrived at the zigzag trail. She quickly began to walk upward, her heart thumping loudly.

Janis was about halfway up the pathway when she heard the sound of footsteps behind her. She resisted the impulse to turn around for fear that she would be completely immobilized with terror if she saw who was following her.

She instinctively quickened her stride, and the person behind her did the same. She could hear the sound of heavy breathing and then she realized it was the sound of her own breath, erratic and labored.

Finally, Janis began to run, no longer caring that the person following her knew that she was aware of his or her presence. Once Janis fell and scraped her knee against some jagged rock. She was on her feet almost immediately and continued to run. By now her lungs felt as though they would burst.

At last she had reached the top of the cliff and she ran frantically ahead. Before her she could dimly make out the shape of Winter House, which had only a few lights on the side facing the ocean. She tried to listen for the footsteps behind her, but her pounding heart blocked out all other sounds. Onward she ran. Her pursuer might be gaining on her and she could not slacken her speed.

After what seemed forever she saw the kitchen door ahead of her. If only she could make it safely. With a last burst of energy Janis ran to the door and flung it open. Then she collapsed on the cold floor.

CHAPTER NINE

"Janis! Are you all right? What happened?" Mary Lee asked in a worried voice.

Janis moved to an upright position and looked into the young girl's concerned face. Mary Lee was kneeling beside her and Janis just sat there for a moment or two, getting her wind back.

"I'm all right, Mary Lee," she finally said when she could trust her voice. "Quick, look out the door and see if anyone is outside."

Mary Lee obediently moved to the door and looked outside. When she came back, she was shaking her head. "There's nobody out there. Should there be?"

"I was down by the beach and it grew dark. After a while, I got the feeling that I was being watched. As I started up the trail to the top of the cliff, I heard somebody behind me. The faster I moved, the faster whoever was behind me moved."

Janis could see that what she was saying terrified Mary Lee, whose eyes were wide with fright.

"Finally, I just ran to the house. When I got here, I just couldn't run any further."

"But who was it? Who was following you?"

Janis shook her head. "I don't know. I was too frightened to look behind me. It was like a nightmare."

She could see the look of puzzlement on Mary Lee's face and she quickly said, "You do believe me, don't you?"

A quick smile spread across Mary Lee's face and her eyes showed that she did not doubt what Janis had told her.

"Of course, I believe you," Mary Lee said. "What a terrible thing to happen to you. First there was that awful voice on the tape and then the lights going out and that man at the window. I don't believe that you are making any of this up. But why, Janis? Why is this person picking on you?"

Janis used one stiff arm and got to her feet. She was still a little wobbly and managed to get to a chair by the table. "I wish I knew. I have no idea why all these things have been happening."

"Can I get you a cup of coffee?"

"That would help," Janis said even though she felt she had had more than her share of coffee for that night.

As Mary Lee hurried over for a cup, Janis ran a hand through her hair, which was tangled. "I must look a mess."

Mary Lee glanced over her shoulder and said, "I'll bring you a comb."

After Mary Lee had brought Janis the coffee and fetched a comb, Janis felt better. She combed her hair and sipped some coffee.

The fright that she had experienced earlier had been replaced by another emotion, anger. She was angry at the person who was making her life such a misery while she was here at Winter House. There was just no excuse for what had been happening to her.

"That's better," Mary Lee said as she sat down at the table with a cup cradled in her hands. "You don't look nearly so much like a whipped puppy now."

"Thanks," Janis said, handing Mary Lee her comb. "And I don't intend to be a whipped puppy any longer. Whoever is doing these things to me had better stop. And even if he continues, I'm not leaving Winter House."

"Do you think that's what he or she wants?" Mary Lee said. "For you to leave Winter House?"

"You heard the tape. It's pretty obvious, isn't it? For some reason somebody doesn't want me here. But I was asked to come here by Clifford Green to do a book and that's what I intend to do. And I'm not leaving until I finish what I came here for."

"Good for you," Mary Lee said as she thumped her coffee cup on the table. "That's exactly the way Elyse would handle things."

"Oh, dear," Janis said with a deep sigh. "I hope I'm more grown-up than Elyse."

"You are. It's just that everything that seems to be happening to you is like something out of a book."

"Well, this is one book I don't want to write. Who needs all this aggravation?"

They were still sitting there when the door to the

kitchen opened from the corridor and Tim Roark walked in.

"Sorry about having to leave you like that, Janis. What Dolores had to say really wasn't that important."

"Oh, Mr. Roark," Mary Lee said as she got to her feet. "You don't know what happened to Janis."

A slight scowl etched itself between Tim's thick eyebrows. "What do you mean?"

"You tell him, Janis," Mary Lee said. "I should check on Mother. She hasn't been feeling very well today."

After Mary Lee had gone, Tim walked over to where Janis was sitting and said, "Now what's Mary Lee going on about? Are you all right?"

"I'm fine. Now. But I can't say the same for a little while ago."

Tim stood before her, his eyes narrowed into tiny slits. For a moment she hesitated to say anything to him about what had happened on the cliff. But Mary Lee had left her no choice.

"After you and Dolores left me, I wandered down that pathway that led to the sea. I must have been there for just a few minutes and I got this strange feeling that somebody was watching me."

Janis hesitated. In the warm, friendly light of the kitchen, the whole episode at the beach seemed unreal.

"Go on," Tim said, still standing there like a rigid statue.

"Well, I felt very uneasy so I started back up the beach to the cliff. All the time I kept looking around, but I didn't see anyone. Then as I began to climb the cliff, I heard someone behind me."

"Who was it?"

Janis felt uncomfortable under his deep scrutiny. She almost felt as though she were being interrogated by the authorities.

"I don't know. I was in too much of a hurry to get away from the beach to look. But I know someone was following me."

"If you didn't look back, how can you be sure of that?"

"I heard whoever it was. I was afraid to look back for fear of stumbling over a rock or the undergrowth. And I was just plain scared to look. When I got to the top, I just kept on running."

"And whoever was following you did the same?"

Janis nodded. "I could hear whoever it was gaining on me. But I made it to the house ahead of him or her. That's about it."

The scowl disappeared from Tim's face and there was a faint, almost amused look in his eyes. "At least you made it back safe and sound."

"No thanks to whoever was following me."

Tim pivoted and started to walk out of the kitchen.

"Where are you going?" Janis asked anxiously.

"To find Lucas. Maybe we won't be too late. Your mysterious person might still be on the property."

Janis got quickly to her feet. Even though she felt a little unsteady, she followed Tim out of the kitchen. "Do you suppose it was the same person I saw through the window in the dining room?"

Tim glanced over his shoulder at Janis. "It might be. At any rate, I think Lucas and I should take a look around."

They found Lucas in the library. Dolores was with him. When she saw Tim, a smile touched her pouty lips. But it crumbled when she saw Janis behind him.

"Come on, Lucas, we're going outside," Tim said.

Lucas yawned and stretched his legs. "Outside? Are you crazy? It's dark out there. Why should we go outside again?"

Tim's exasperation showed in his tone of voice. "Janis was followed by someone when she was at the beach."

"Now, really, Tim," Dolores said without trying to disguise the scorn in her voice. "This is going a bit far. You can come up with a better story than that."

Janis had been expecting something like that from Dolores. But her voice, when she spoke, was calm and level.

"I didn't make it up. Any more than I made up that man I saw in the dining-room window."

Lucas got to his feet. "At least tell me who we are looking for and what happened to Janis."

"Tell him, Janis," Tim said as he impatiently tapped his foot against the carpet on the floor.

Janis went over the story for the third time. As she related what had happened to her along the cliff, she saw that Dolores's mouth twisted in a mocking smirk. Lucas's face was an unfathomable mask, but at least he was listening to what she had to say.

When she finished, Lucas said, "So you didn't get a look at whoever it was?"

"Sorry, but I was just concentrating on the trail. I was afraid that if I did look, I might trip over something and fall. Or I didn't want to see who it was. All I could think of was getting away from that place and to the safety of the house."

"I can't blame you for that," Tim said, and Janis

began to feel reassured.

"I'll go with you," Lucas said. "But by this time, our phantom is probably miles away from here."

"Don't be too sure about that," Janis said. "If he didn't go away after I saw him in the window, he might still be out there hiding someplace."

Dolores sighed and said, "This is just too ridiculous to believe. Honestly, Tim, can't you see that Miss Long is just imagining things? Lucas didn't see anyone at the window. And Janis herself says that she didn't see anyone on the trail. This is all just a lot of wasted effort on both your and Lucas's part."

Janis had taken just about enough from Dolores. She turned and faced Tim. "Believe her if you want to. But I know what I saw in the dining room and I know that someone was on that trail behind me. If you and Lucas don't want to go and search for whoever it is, I will."

A gentle laugh came from Tim and he reached out and took Janis's shoulders in his strong hands. "Now don't get all riled up. Lucas and I are going out there. And I want you to stay inside with Dolores until we come back. It wouldn't be a bad idea for you to lock the doors while we are gone."

"Whatever you say, Tim," Dolores said, getting Tim's attention back from Janis. "But I would suggest that if you and Lucas are going, you start now. If we keep this up, it will be daylight before you two leave the house."

"Let's go, Lucas," Tim said as he released his hold on Janis's shoulders. "But first let's get some flashlights."

After the two men had gone, Dolores reached out and made an over-obvious gesture at locking the front door. "There, does that suit you, Miss Scaredy-Cat?"

Janis had never felt more like reaching out and shaking anyone in her entire life. It took all the restraint she could summon to keep from doing just that.

"You don't believe me, do you, Dolores?"

"Oh, I believe you were followed. But it wasn't by some phantom. It was either a dog or a jackrabbit."

Janis couldn't believe what Dolores was saying. "It wasn't an animal that was out there. I know the difference."

Dolores arched a skeptical eyebrow. "Do you? I'm beginning to wonder about you."

"What do you mean?" Janis asked.

"It's just that it's very odd. There was nothing like this happening here before you arrived. You come on the scene, and suddenly there are ghosts all over the place. That's what I mean."

Janis stared at Dolores. The woman returned her gaze with haughty eyes.

"Believe me, I don't want all this happening to me. I just came to Winter House to do a book for Clifford Green. But if you or anyone else here think they can frighten me away, they've got another think coming. I do not frighten easily."

"That's too bad," Dolores said. "If I were in your position, I would be terribly frightened."

"Then you admit there is something for me to be frightened of."

"Just yourself," Dolores said in a cold, deadly tone of voice. "If I were you, I would pack my things and head right back to New York. Oregon just isn't the right place for you to be in."

"That sounds like a warning to me," Janis said, not

letting Dolores intimidate her.

"Take it for what you will. Excuse me," Dolores said as she turned and walked away.

Janis stared after Dolores until she had turned the corner of the corridor and walked out of sight. That was the second warning she had been given since she had arrived at Winter House. Could Dolores be the person responsible for all that had happened to her since she had arrived only a short time ago? She didn't need a house to fall on her to know that the woman despised her. She wouldn't put it past Dolores to want her out of Winter House so desperately that she would resort to any and all measures.

Hurrying down the hallway, Janis went to the back door and locked it as Tim had advised her. Then she went into the library and waited for Tim and Lucas to return. It was a long, tension-filled hour before she heard the loud banging on the front door and she hurried there to let Tim and Lucas in.

"Nobody," Tim said, and he glanced skeptically at Lucas, who just yawned and excused himself. After he had gone, Tim said, "I'll be running along. It's been a long and tiring night. You watch your step while you're here, understand?"

"I understand. Thanks for all you and Lucas did for me tonight."

"That's all right. Just call me if there is any more trouble. Will you do that?"

"I promise," Janis said as she closed the door behind Tim.

Standing there in the corridor, Janis once again felt she was being observed. She turned her head in the direction of the kitchen. Jonas was standing in the doorway. Suddenly, he turned and shut the kitchen door behind him.

Janis knew that he had been watching her, and a faint chill eased its way down her spine as she hurried up the staircase.

CHAPTER TEN

Janis locked the door to her room after she had entered it. She could still see the expression on Jonas's face before he turned and went into the kitchen. It was the gardener's eyes more than anything else that bothered her. Jonas had looked at her as though he had some secret that he was keeping.

After Janis had slipped between the covers on her bed, she lay there with the lamp on, staring at the ceiling. The house was once again quiet and she had the feeling that she was the only person in the huge place. At first she found that sleep was impossible, although her body cried out for rest.

If only she had taken that split second it would have required to turn and see who was pursuing her. Then, perhaps she would rest easier at Winter House. And then, again, perhaps she might be lying now at the base of the cliff, the victim of the person who had chased her.

Janis finally shut the light and tried to close her eyes. But she tossed and turned for a long time before she fell into a deep sleep.

When she awoke the next morning, Janis lay still for a few minutes, getting her thoughts in order. There was something about today, something special, that she was trying to remember. Then it dawned on her. Tim had asked her to go with him to see the rain forest. Janis quickly threw back the covers on the bed and raced to the shower. Its prickling force awakened her, and she quickly dressed in jeans and a sweater.

She took a few minutes to sit before her mirror and brush her blond hair. Then she lightly applied some gloss to her lips and studied her face.

"I'm no competition for Dolores," she sighed but didn't let that interfere with her anticipation of being with Tim.

She hurried out of the room and down the stairs to the dining room. When she entered it, she found that she was all alone. This was a relief because Janis did not feel like facing Dolores so early in the day. She helped herself to a cup of coffee and a toasted English muffin.

As she sat there, munching on the muffin and taking sips of the coffee, she thought about the Elyse book and how she would illustrate it. The pictures were beginning to take vague shape in her mind and she was eager to put them on her sketching pad. This she would do when she returned from her outing with Tim.

Janis was at the sideboard refilling her cup with coffee when Dolores walked in.

"Good morning," Dolores said in a cold voice. "Did you have a good night's rest? Or were there bogeymen in your room last night?"

Janis let the words slide past her. "I slept very well, thank you."

"You're up early. What are your plans for the day? Are you going to do one of your works of art?"

"As a matter of fact, no. Tim and I are going to the rain forest today. He thought I would enjoy seeing it."

"I'll bet," Dolores said.

"The book has a scene in the woods," Janis said. "I might be able to use the rain forest for that."

"How nice," Dolores said sarcastically. Then she walked briskly out of the room.

Janis was getting used to Dolores's rudeness and she merely shrugged after the statuesque beauty had left. She knew that she might miss the beauty of Oregon when she went back to New York, but she certainly would not miss seeing Dolores Webster. Janis usually got along very well with women. She had a few close female friends back in New York. But Dolores Webster was certainly something else.

Tim came before nine, but Janis did not mind in the least.

"Shall I apologize for being early?" he said, and a lazy smile spread across his lips.

"Not to me," Janis said. "I've been looking forward to seeing the rain forest ever since you mentioned it."

"Good," Tim said as he took her arm and led her out of the house and to his car. "It isn't very far, and you couldn't ask for a better day to see the rain forest."

"But it's overcast," Janis said, glancing up at the gauzy veils of cloud that filled the sky.

"That's what I mean. Nice and gloomy. Just the right sort of day for a trip into the distant past," Tim said and then chuckled. "Did you have a good night's rest?"

"Sort of. When I finally did get to sleep, I really slept."

"You've been having a pretty rough time of it since you arrived at Winter House, haven't you?"

"There have been things happening, yes. But I'm not going to leave until I finish what I came here to do. I'm going back to New York with my illustrations tucked underneath my arm."

Again Tim chuckled. "I'll say one thing for you, Janis Long. You are tenacious."

"Stubborn might be a better word for it. I get that from my dad. He never gives up on anything either. Sort of runs in the family."

"I think I would like your father," Tim said as he cast a quick glance in Janis's direction.

"What are your parents like?"

There was a brief pause as Tim concentrated on the road ahead of them. Then he said, "They're both dead. My father died of a heart attack a few years ago, worked himself into it. A year later my mother died of pneumonia."

"I'm sorry," Janis said. "Have you any brothers or sisters?"

"Just me. I have a couple of aunts and uncles and some cousins scattered across the country. But we haven't kept up a close relationship."

Janis's heart went out to Tim. In a way he was all alone in the world. It was sad that he did not have anyone close to him.

Then Tim changed the subject and the seriousness left him. He could be a witty and clever conversationalist when he chose to be. And he was very knowledgeable about almost everything. By the time they arrived at the rain forest, they were both in a relaxed, happy frame of mind.

The forest was awesome to Janis. Trees and ferns and other greenery grew to a great height, closing out the cloudy sky, and she found herself shivering in the cool green dampness.

"Hey, are you cold?" Tim said, unzipping his windbreaker.

"A little bit," Janis said as Tim removed the windbreaker and slipped it over her shoulders. She would have protested, but the jacket did make her feel warmer and Tim did not seem the least bit uncomfortable without it.

They were the only ones in their section of the forest and it gave Janis an eerie feeling. Suddenly, she glanced to her right and she gave out a startled shriek. Then she realized what she had seen was just an artificial prehistoric monster that had been built to give authenticity to the forest.

"Don't worry, fair lady," Tim said. "I'll protect you."

Janis stood there laughing as he ran up to the beast and took a boxer's stance. Then Tim climbed up the side of the statue and took a triumphant seat on its back. He motioned for Janis to join him, but she declined. Tim climbed down and walked back to her.

"My hero," Janis said, batting her eyelashes in a coy manner.

They both laughed and continued their stroll through the forest.

"What do you think of it?" Tim asked as they paused to rest a little later.

"It has a wild, untamed beauty about it," Janis said. "But it's peaceful here and serene. Kind of like Winter House might be."

"Might be?" Tim said.

"If it wasn't for all the trouble that's going on there," Janis said with a sigh.

"Trouble or not, I'd like to own that house," Tim said, and there was a touch of bitterness in his voice.

"Winter House? You want to buy it? But you already have a house."

"My place was second choice. When I saw Winter House, I knew that was the place I had been searching for. But I couldn't persuade Clifford Green to sell it."

Janis glanced at Tim. His face was hard-looking in the dim light of the forest. "You mean you've approached Clifford to sell you Winter House?"

Tim emitted a bitter chuckle. "Not just once, but many times. I'd do just about anything to get my hands on that house. But Clifford Green is just as stubborn as I am persistent. He flatly refuses any offer I've made. And I can tell you they have been generous offers. However, there are ways to get him to change his mind."

Janis did not like this side of Tim Roark. His jawline was taut and there was a coldness in his eyes that frightened her. She could believe that Tim would stop at nothing to get what he wanted. It was as though she were standing next to a stranger.

"Let's move on," Tim said. "If you are rested enough."

Janis welcomed the opportunity to change the scenery

and the tone of the conversation. But as they walked quietly along the path, she felt as though all the joy and fun had gone out of the morning. The forest had suddenly become oppressive and dark. She tried to bring herself out of this mood, but somehow it was futile.

Tim sensed her mood and his conversation became lighter and more humorous. Slowly Janis felt the oppression leave her, and even found herself laughing at Tim and his antics.

The trail they followed circled back to the entrance of the forest. As they neared the place where they had parked the car, Janis saw that other people had begun to arrive. She welcomed the presence of them since the gigantic trees and ferns were beginning to overpower her.

There was a small lodge near the entrance which sold curios and picture postcards.

"I think I'll send my folks a card," Janis said as they neared the place.

"Go ahead and find one," Tim said. "There's something I have to get out of the car. I'll join you in a few minutes."

Janis entered the lodge and began idly riffling through a rack of postcards. She found several she liked and went to the glass-topped counter to pay for them. The clerk was friendly and they chatted for a few minutes.

Then Janis turned to walk to the door, and she saw someone standing in the doorway. At first, because the light was in her eyes, she thought it was Tim. But as she moved closer, she saw that she had been mistaken.

Glaring at her—smiling his crooked smile—was Floyd Phillips. Janis paused in her tracks. The postcards she was holding dropped to the floor. Hurriedly she gathered them in her hands and then stood up.

But the figure in the doorway was gone. Floyd Phillips had mysteriously vanished.

CHAPTER ELEVEN

"Janis! What happened? Are you all right?"

It took her a few moments to realize that it was Tim who was speaking to her.

"I guess I'm all right," Janis managed to say in a shaky voice.

"You look as though you've seen a ghost."

"I don't believe in ghosts," Janis said. "And what I saw was certainly a very real person."

"Let's get out of here," Tim said. "Did you get everything that you wanted?"

Janis held up the handful of cards. "This is all that I wanted."

She felt Tim's strong hand on her elbow as he escorted her out of the lodge. Once Janis was outside, she took a deep breath of the chilly, damp air and her head cleared itself entirely. She glanced quickly around to see if Floyd was anywhere in sight, but she knew that he had a head start and was probably hiding somewhere watching her.

Tim did not say anything as they walked the short distance to the car, but Janis felt that his eyes were upon her as she kept glancing furtively around. At the moment, she didn't care what Tim thought. If only she could get another glimpse of Floyd Phillips. Then she would be certain it was he she had seen at the motel.

When they got to Tim's car, he opened the door on the passenger side and thoughtfully helped her inside. Janis would have protested, but at the moment she was too busy trying to see if she could spot Floyd. There were just too many places for him to hide in the overgrown forest. The outing, which had started out to be such fun, had turned into a nightmare.

Tim closed the door on Janis's side and then walked over to the driver's side and slipped behind the wheel.

"Do you want to talk about it? Or do you want to wait a while?"

"Later, please," Janis said as Tim turned the key in the ignition.

Even as they drove away, she kept looking for any sign of Floyd. She knew that she hadn't been mistaken this time. This time she had actually seen Floyd. All of her suspicions had been well grounded. Floyd had followed her from New York. He had been the one she had seen in the motel parking lot that night.

Floyd had made threats against her and evidently he intended to carry them out.

Janis suddenly became aware that the car had taken her and Tim away from the rain forest. The scenery outside the car was familiar to her. She turned and looked at Tim, who was concentrating on the road ahead.

"You probably would like an explanation for the way I acted back there," Janis said.

"I am curious, yes," Tim replied.

Janis took a deep breath, then said, "When I was working in New York, I met this man. His name is Phillips, Floyd Phillips. As far as I was concerned, we were just friends. And that was the way Floyd accepted our relationship. For a time, that is. Then he gradually became more and more possessive and jealous."

Tim said nothing. He just listened intently.

"I tried to explain to Floyd that I did not care for him in the same way he cared for me. If he wanted to remain friends with me, that was all right. But I was not in love with him and I made that perfectly clear to him. Then he became more and more jealous. There were scenes in restaurants and it got to the point where I decided that I just couldn't continue with Floyd. So I told him that he shouldn't see me anymore."

"What did he have to say about that?" Tim asked.

"He threatened me, said something foolish like if he couldn't have me, nobody else would either," Janis said.

"That sounds like dangerous talk to me," Tim said.

"It was just that, talk. Or so I thought. But one night when I was on my way here to Winter House, I thought I saw Floyd in the parking lot of the motel I was staying in. I didn't get a good look at him, so I couldn't be entirely sure that it was Floyd."

"Go on," Tim said.

"Then today, at the lodge, I saw Floyd. He was

standing in the doorway just as I was about to leave. I was so startled that I dropped the cards I was holding. After I'd picked them up, I looked at the doorway, but Floyd was gone."

Tim looked at Janis for a second and then shifted his eyes back to the road. "Maybe it was just somebody who looked like Floyd."

"No, it was Floyd, all right. I was close enough to see him clearly. He was standing there with that same crooked smile on his face. That smile he used whenever he was planning something."

"Why do you suppose he followed you all the way to Oregon?"

"If you knew Floyd, you wouldn't have to ask that question. That's the kind of person he is. When he feels he has been wronged, he'll stop at nothing to get even with a person."

"But what about his job? He does work, doesn't he?"

Janis nodded. "He owns a camera store in New York. But he has reliable people working for him. It wouldn't be any problem for him to take off and come to Oregon."

There was a rest stop ahead of them and Tim pulled off the side of the road. "We can't let all this food I prepared go to waste. Are you hungry?"

Janis wasn't, but she did not want to hurt Tim's feelings. "The view is breathtaking from up here. And you did go to all that trouble."

Tim opened the door for Janis and got out the hamper that was in the back seat. He led her to a level spot of ground that was surrounded by a cluster of rocks and they sat down.

Even though Janis was not hungry, she managed to pick at the fried chicken and sip the coffee Tim had poured into a plastic cup. Tim was so busy eating that he did not notice how little Janis ate. From time to time, she saw him glance at the road.

"This Floyd character, you are certain that you didn't give him any encouragement?"

Janis said, "Of course, I'm certain. At first Floyd was very friendly and just the sort of person I needed at the time for a friend. I never in any way gave him any encouragement. As a matter of fact, I kept reminding him that all I could be to him was a friend."

"Apparently, he thought otherwise," Tim said, then took a bite of chicken.

"You must believe me, Tim," Janis said with as much force as she could muster. "At first he was fine and then he just changed overnight. If we were out having dinner and I happened to look at another man, he would create a scene. It got so bad that finally I just would not go to dinner with him."

"I believe you," Tim said. "I guess he was just mixed up. Couldn't take no for an answer."

"Yes. I'd hoped that maybe coming out here to Oregon would be good for both of us. That he would have time to find someone else. And it would be good for me to be away from Floyd. But it hasn't worked out that way."

"It doesn't seem so."

"If Floyd followed me here, then that explains everything."

"Everything?"

"You know, the tape that was in my room. Whoever

was at the dining-room window. And that explains who it was that followed me when I was down by the ocean last night."

Tim asked, "So you think it was Floyd Phillips that you saw last night?"

"Who else could it be?"

He shrugged. "Makes sense. Only, I can't quite make myself believe that it could be him."

"You don't know him, Tim. Floyd Phillips is capable of just about anything."

"Well, he's certainly gone to a whole lot of trouble to make life miserable for you."

Janis leaned back against a rock. "That's the way Floyd Phillips thinks. He really should get some psychiatric help. His jealousy is consuming him. If it wasn't for that and his possessiveness, he would be a very fine person. In a way, I feel sorry for him."

"I can see how you would."

Janis glanced at Tim just to reassure herself that he was not being cynical. She certainly could not tell that from his face. It was a stoical mask.

"What do you mean?" she asked.

"Just that you are a very special, sensitive person," he said warmly. "I admire that in you. The more I get to know you, the better I get to like you."

"Thank you," Janis said. "That's nice to hear."

"I admire a lot of people and a lot of things," Tim went on.

Suddenly, the warmth was gone. In its place was an almost smug tone that Janis did not particularly care for.

"Such as Winter House?" she asked.

Tim nodded. "For one. I still can't see why Clifford Green is so obstinate. Can't he see that Winter House would be perfect for me?"

Janis said, "Well, after all, it is his house and he can do whatever he wants with it."

A dark look crept across Tim's handsome face. "He's never at Winter House. What earthly good does it do him to own the place? Now if it were mine, it would be a different story."

"In what way?"

"I'd make it a home . . . not a museum piece. The way Winter House is now, it's like living in the Smithsonian Institution. Who can be comfortable in a place full of antiques?"

"Apparently, Clifford Green, for one, can," Janis said, turning to look at the surrounding scenery.

"You are wrong there. Clifford Green doesn't live in Winter House. I doubt if he sees the place once in three years. To Clifford Green, Winter House is just a nice tax write-off. Certainly not a home."

By this time Janis was beginning to tire of the subject of Winter House and maybe just a little of Tim Roark's obsession with it. Still, she did not say anything. Instead, she tried to concentrate on the beautiful landscape that spread out beyond them. But it really wasn't any good. Somehow Janis found her mind being drawn back to Tim Roark and what he was saying.

"Yes, if I could get my hands on Winter House, you'd see a definite change in the place," he sighed.

Tim looked at Janis. "I have an uncomfortable feeling that you haven't been listening to a word I've been saying."

Janis met his unblinking stare with open-eyed sincerity. "Of course, I have. You have made it very clear that you want Winter House in the worst way."

"That's right. And I intend on getting the place. Somehow or some way Clifford Green will eventually sell that house to me."

"Clifford Green can be a very stubborn man," Janis said, drawing on some of her past experience with the publisher.

"But I can be just as stubborn," Tim said.

Janis stared at Tim as he shifted his gaze from her and once again concentrated on the road.

There didn't seem to be anything further that they could discuss. Tim wanted Winter House, wanted it so badly it was consuming him. Janis wondered just how far he would go to obtain the place. Was it possible that Tim wanted the house so badly that he had been the person behind what had happened to her since she had arrived in Oregon? But that just couldn't be, Janis said to herself. It had to be Floyd Phillips.

Floyd was the one who had somehow put the tape in her room and then had returned for it through the open window. He had been the one who had been standing by the dining-room window staring at her while she was sitting with Lucas. And he most definitely had been the person who had followed her from the beach to the house.

Yet, was Floyd also the one who had brushed past her on the stairs, deliberately trying to make her fall down? Janis figured that it was possible he might have been hiding somewhere in the house and had used that darkened interval to make his escape from the place.

"Ready to go?" Tim said, jarring Janis out of her reverie.

"Whenever you are," she replied, and Tim helped her to her feet.

Together they carried the remains of the picnic lunch back to the car. They both took one final look at where they had been sitting and then Janis got into the car.

In a way, she hated to see this trip end. It had been a peaceful time up here, even though Tim had revealed how much he wanted to own Clifford Green's home. She glanced out the window at their picnic spot and wondered if she would ever see the place again.

Don't be so sentimental, Janis said to herself. You'll be gone from this place in a few weeks and it is very doubtful that you will ever return again. So don't get too attached to anything around here.

Tim drove away. Apparently, his thoughts were somewhere else, for he did not so much as look at the site where they had had their picnic.

They were getting closer to Winter House when Tim suddenly turned to Janis and said, "We've been followed ever since we left the rain forest."

"So that's why you kept looking at the road. You knew all the time that someone was following us. Do you think it's Floyd Phillips?"

Tim didn't have to answer that. Janis knew it couldn't be anyone else.

CHAPTER TWELVE

"He's not there anymore," Tim said as they pulled into the Winter House drive. "He must have suspected that we were on to him."

Janis turned in her seat and glanced out the rear window. If Floyd Phillips had been following them, he wasn't any longer. There was no other car visible on the road behind them.

Tim braked the car but left the engine idle. "You go on inside. I'm going to drive back to the main road and see if I can find that car."

"Be careful," Janis said as she opened the door and got out.

"I can take care of myself," Tim said, releasing the brake. "You just watch your step while you're at Winter House. I'll be keeping an eye on the house just in case Floyd Phillips decides to make another appearance."

With that Tim stepped on the accelerator and was gone. Janis stood there for a moment or two until Tim's car vanished around a curve in the road. She was deeply concerned for him. Even though, physically, Floyd was no match for Tim, Floyd was very cunning and possibly dangerous. Janis silently prayed Tim would not be harmed. Then she walked toward the house.

She went directly to her room without seeing anyone. In order to keep her mind off Tim and Floyd, she got out her sketch pad. She sat at the desk and began to draw whatever came into her mind. That went on for about an hour and then she set aside the pad and her charcoal, and looked at what she had been sketching.

There was nothing here that could be used in the Elyse book. What Janis had drawn was how Winter House had looked during one of her nightmares. There she was running frantically through the huge house as though someone were pursuing her. The sketches were frightening and she tore them into tiny pieces.

Time and again she went to the window and peered out, half thinking that she would see either Tim or Floyd on the grounds below. She did not even see the beautiful scenery. At any other time she would have admired the view but not now. She was too upset by her thoughts of Floyd. Had Tim caught up with him? If so, was Tim all right?

By the time Janis went down to dinner, she had worked herself into a state of nerves. Just as she was about to enter the dining room, Mary Lee came hurrying up to her.

"Telephone, Janis. It's Mr. Roark."

Janis took quick steps into the library and picked up the extension. It was reassuring to hear Tim's voice on the other end of the line.

"I lost Floyd. For a stranger to these parts, he certainly knows his way around. I just thought I'd call you and let you know what's been happening."

Janis was relieved to hear that Tim was all right even though she was concerned about Floyd and what he might be planning next.

"You just stay inside the house tonight, Janis. Don't go on any long walks. I'll be watching the house, but there's no need of you deliberately asking for trouble."

Assuring Tim that she had no intention of going out tonight, she hung up. Janis felt better and more relaxed after she had spoken to Tim. At times like these she felt that he was being totally honest with her.

But there were other times when—well, she wouldn't think about that right now.

Now that she had spoken to Tim, she knew she would be able to eat tonight. As Janis walked into the dining room, she found that her appetite had indeed returned. Dolores and Lucas were talking in low voices and when they saw Janis they broke off their conversation. Dolores smiled at Janis and that in itself was enough to make her suspicious of the tall, statuesque beauty.

"How was your visit to the rain forest?" Dolores asked in a syrupy-sweet voice.

"Very interesting and enjoyable," Janis said, taking a seat at the table. "Tim is a very knowledgeable and amusing guide."

Janis studied Dolores's face and saw just a faint twitching of the woman's mouth, but otherwise she appeared not to be ruffled by what Janis had said.

"Isn't he, though?" Dolores said. "I'll have to ask

him to take me on a tour of the forest one of these days. Now that he comes so highly recommended."

Janis didn't reply as Winnifred had entered with the food. Turning to the housekeeper, Janis commented on how good everything looked and how tantalizing the aromas were.

Winnifred sighed as she paused by Janis's chair. "Thanks, Miss Long. I truly appreciate that. But you know I have this longing to really cook up a storm. You know, for a large group of people. Not that you all aren't hearty eaters."

"That is a coincidence," Dolores said as she leaned forward. "Lucas and I were just talking about having a party here at Winter House. You might just get your wish, Winnifred."

"A party? Here at Winter House?" Winnifred said and her voice seemed excited.

"That's right," Dolores said. And then she looked across the table directly into Janis's eyes. "Unless, of course, Miss Long has any objection."

"Why should I object?" Janis said. "What do I have to do with your plans?"

Lucas turned his gold-flecked eyes on Janis. "Have you forgotten your conversation with my father? Winter House is under your guidance while you remain here. That's what he told me. And I'm sure that he conveyed that message to you also."

Janis felt uncomfortable under the unblinking eyes of both Dolores and Lucas. "He couldn't have meant that I have control over the activities that go on here."

Lucas raised one eyebrow. "I'm very certain that he did, Miss Long. You really don't know my father as well as I do. When he told me that you were to have the run of the house while you were here, that is exactly what he meant."

"So you see, Miss Long," Dolores said with sugary tones, "we really can't have a party here unless you are in agreement."

Janis glanced up at Winnifred, who was the only one in the room not looking at her with critical eyes. "Are you sure you want to cook for a bunch of strangers, Winnifred?"

Winnifred's face brightened with a wide smile. "Mr. Green used to bring a whole gaggle of friends with him whenever he visited Winter House. This would be like that."

"If you don't think it will be too much of a burden on you, Winnifred, then I really have no objection," Janis said and she could see the relieved looks on both Lucas and Dolores's faces.

"That's very considerate of you," Dolores said with just a touch of her usual venom.

Winnifred glared briefly at the statuesque brunette before departing.

"What kind of party will it be?" Janis asked. "And who will be here?"

"Just some of my friends," Dolores said. "I've already called them. They'll be arriving in a few days."

"Do we have room for all of them to stay over?" Janis asked.

"My friends?" Dolores laughed. "As soon as this party ends, they'll be off to another one. They sleep whenever they get a chance."

Inwardly Janis already disliked Dolores's friends. She had run into such people in New York. The bored rich. Very shallow and surface people. Janis was already beginning to dread meeting them. But it came as no surprise to her they would be the sort of people that Dolores would find fascinating.

Janis left Lucas and Dolores sitting at the table discussing the plans for the party as she went to her room. She spent the next few hours at her desk and for once she was productive. Working on the sketches kept her mind off Floyd Phillips and Tim Roark and Dolores and her party.

At about nine o'clock, Janis took a warm bath and then slipped beneath the covers on the bed. She gathered the sketches she had done earlier around her so that she could study them before she went to sleep. She glanced at them with satisfaction. They really were very good and she had captured the feeling of the new Elyse book.

Then Janis put the sketches aside and lay back on the pillows. Somehow she had forced herself not to think about Floyd Phillips, but now that she was alone and resting, she could no longer push him out of her mind.

She wondered what Floyd was doing at that very moment. Was he skulking around the gardens somewhere? Was he watching her room at this very moment? It gave Janis a cold chill to think of Floyd standing outside and staring up at her window. She reached out and with a touch pitched the room into darkness.

It was difficult for Janis to fall asleep that night, but eventually she did. Yet her dreams were all about Floyd Philips and how sinister he could be.

Several days later Dolores began the preparations for the party, which was to be held that evening. She seemed a different woman rushing around making sure that Mary Lee was dusting and cleaning properly. She was even mildly friendly to Janis, which was a relief after the coldness she had been displaying since Janis had arrived at Winter House.

During the day Janis helped as best she could, trying to keep peace between Dolores and Winnifred.

"Look, Miss Long," Winnifred said to Janis when they were both in the kitchen. "I've catered to a lot of parties in my day. And like I said, I really enjoy cooking for a lot of people. But that Miss Webster is beginning to get my goat. She's done everything but put salt and pepper in my Swedish meatballs."

"Don't let her upset you, Winnifred," Janis said in a soothing tone. "She's just excited about her friends coming."

"If it was you giving the orders, I wouldn't mind one little bit," Winnifred said. "But I'll try to do my very best. Only, I got a feeling about this party. I just don't think it will be a success."

"Let's hope for the best," Janis said, and Winnifred managed a feeble smile before the girl left the kitchen.

But, as Winnifred had predicted, for Janis the party was not a success. By eight o'clock the guests had all arrived. It was obvious from the first that they were all in a clique. No outsider would be admitted unless that person was accepted by everyone and particularly Dolores.

"Don't look so downcast, Janis," Tim said, startling her as she stood near the living-room fireplace. "This can't be all that bad."

"Do I show it that much?" Janis asked as she looked up into Tim's dark brown eyes.

He was wearing a tan sports coat and brown slacks

and he looked more handsome than ever. A fact that was not wasted on any of the unattached females at the party.

Before Tim could answer, he was swept away by a couple who had heard about his work as an architect, leaving Janis once again feeling alone and left out.

Lucas ambled over to her and he appeared to be drinking quite heavily.

"Well, Miss Long, you don't seem to be enjoying yourself. My, my, what would my esteemed father have to say about that?"

"I'm enjoying myself," Janis said, trying not to upset Lucas. "Dolores certainly knows how to throw a party."

Lucas glanced around. "She can afford to. Or at least she likes to give that impression. But I know otherwise."

Janis did not say anything. She just waited to hear what Lucas was about to say.

"I happen to know that our Miss Webster is flat broke. This party will just about wipe out what little savings she has."

Janis was shocked at this news. Even though she had never given it much thought, she just assumed that Dolores was well off financially.

"But why is she throwing this party if it'll cost her everything she has?"

"Why does Dolores do anything?" Lucas said with a shrug and walked away.

The evening was getting progressively worse for Janis. She wandered around, trying to join in with the others, but it didn't take her long to learn that she was just not welcomed in Dolores's circle of friends.

Janis found herself by the French windows of the

living room and she walked outside. There was no moon tonight. It was hidden somewhere in the heavy bank of clouds. The night was just as dark as Janis's mood. She glanced back at the party that was going on inside and she heard the laughter that only added to her depression.

Unmindful of where she was going, Janis began to walk. She wanted to get away from the house for a few minutes, away from the unfriendly guests. If she returned now, she was afraid that she might say something to one of the guests that would reveal how she actually felt about Dolores and them.

Janis's thoughts were on what Lucas had said about Dolores as she casually strolled along the pathway that led from the house toward the ocean. Even though there was a slight breeze, Janis did not feel the cold. She wondered what Tim was doing now. Who was he talking to? He seemed to fit in with that crowd of people. In a way, he seemed to. But Janis also got the impression that Tim was just playing a part. Maybe he was just trying to please Dolores.

Janis was walking further and further away from the house and the laughter and chatter of the guests began to grow fainter. Suddenly, she heard a sound, a faint footfall that brought her sharply out of her reflections. She paused for a moment and listened. She knew that someone was behind her. Slowly Janis turned. She gasped as she saw Floyd Phillips standing in front of her.

CHAPTER THIRTEEN

"Hello, Janis," Floyd said in a low tone.

Janis couldn't trust her own voice. She stood there staring at Floyd, her feet like lead weights.

Finally, she nodded her head. "Hello, Floyd. Why are you here?"

Floyd moved a step towards her and then paused. There was a rift in the clouds and moonlight fell on his face. This was a different Floyd from the one she had remembered. He hadn't shaved recently and his eyes seemed to bore right into her own.

"You know the answer to that. I couldn't let you just walk away from me in New York. I had to follow you. You didn't expect me to remain back there while you were out in Oregon among strangers, did you?"

"But I have work to do here, Floyd. You know that's why I came."

112

"That's what you told me. Only, I don't believe you," Floyd said, and there was a dangerous edge to his voice.

"But it's the truth," Janis said, trying to keep the uneasiness out of her voice.

This was not the Floyd Phillips she had known back in New York. Even though he had been jealous and possessive, he had never looked at her with such cruelty before.

A sudden burst of laughter from the house caused Floyd to turn his head and glance in that direction. When he turned his attention back to Janis, his lips had curled into an unpleasant snarl.

"Let's get away from here, Janis. All of that racket is giving me a headache."

Floyd quickly took her by the arm. She thought of wrenching free and making a dash for the house, but she knew that she was no match for Floyd. He would overtake her in a matter of seconds if she tried anything so foolish.

As they walked, she could feel the viselike grip on her arm. She would have to wait for the right moment and make her escape. She could have cried out, but she knew that she wouldn't be heard above the noise of the guests in the house. And if she tried to call out, that might just upset Floyd even further. So Janis walked beside him, trying as best she could not to show any signs of fright.

"How long have you been here?" Janis asked, making every effort to keep her voice normal.

"Ever since you have been. I followed you all the way across the country. When you stopped, I stopped. When you drove slowly, I drove slowly."

"I understand," Janis said. "Even though you didn't have to do that, Floyd."

"Oh, yes I did. Somebody had to look after you. Somebody had to protect you. You should never have left New York, Janis. Oregon isn't a good place for you."

"Why do you say that?"

"You don't belong here. New York is the place for you. You're not a small-town person."

"That's where you're wrong, Floyd. You know that I grew up in a small town. I haven't always lived in New York. That's just where I work."

Floyd tightened his grip on her arm. "And now you're trying to tell me that you're working here in this isolated place."

"That's right. Clifford Green asked me to come here to do the illustrations for a new book. I told you all that before, Floyd."

Floyd's free hand went to his head and he moved it back and forth as though he were trying to clear cobwebs away from his mind.

"You're not telling me the truth, Janis. That's not the real reason you came here to Winter House."

"What other reason could there be?" she asked.

Floyd was becoming quite agitated now. "Who is he, Janis?"

"What do you mean?"

"You know what I mean. Who are you seeing here at this house? What is the man's name?"

Janis knew that she had to calm Floyd down. There was no telling what he might do in this state of mind.

"You're mistaken, Floyd. There isn't any man, as you put it. I wish that you would understand I'm only at Winter House to do my work. When it is finished, I'll be coming back to New York."

Floyd didn't say anything for a few moments as he guided Janis further and further from the house. She wanted desperately to glance back, but she was afraid that might upset him.

"But I saw you sitting at the table with that man," Floyd said.

Then it *was* Floyd she had seen from the dining room. In a way, she was relieved. At least it wasn't Tim Roark.

"That was Lucas, Clifford Green's son. After all, he lives there. You certainly can't think that I'm interested in him."

"I don't know what to think," Floyd said in a high, quivery voice. "You left New York so unexpectedly."

"But I told you where I was going," Janis said calmly.

"How could I believe you?" Floyd answered. "How can I ever believe what you're saying?"

Janis took another tack.

"You didn't have to leave New York, Floyd. What about your business there?"

"What does it matter?" he said desolately.

"It matters a great deal. You've worked hard for your business. Anything could happen while you're gone."

Floyd shrugged. "Andy Ellis is a good man. He's trustworthy. Besides, I wouldn't be much good back there with you out here in Oregon."

"Floyd, it's kind of you to think of me. But really I'm just fine. And I'm so wrapped up in the book that I can't think of anything else," Janis said, knowing it wasn't the exact truth.

"You're not going to stay here long enough to finish those sketches," Floyd said in a menacing tone of voice.

"What do you mean?"

"I mean that you're going back to New York City. That's where you belong. Not out here in the wilds of Oregon. I can't stand the place."

Janis could hear the sound of the ocean as they neared the cliff. It was impossible for her to even catch one faint whisper of laughter from the house. She tried to think of some way to get free of Floyd. If he would just let go of her arm for a second, she would make a break for it.

"Floyd, please listen to me. I'm not going back to New York City until I have finished what I came here to do. What could I tell Clifford when I got back? After all, I do have a commitment. That's how I earn my money."

Floyd sniffed. "You don't have to work for that man. I don't trust him. There are other book companies, other assignments you could do."

"But I happen to like working on the Elyse books. I do other things for Green Publishing too. And, besides, you're mistaken about Clifford Green. He's a very considerate and thoughtful man. Who else would allow someone to come into their home and use it for a place to work?"

"I am not mistaken about Clifford Green. Nobody is that generous! He's up to something. He's interested in you."

By this time they had almost reached the edge of the high cliff overlooking the ocean. The sound of the pounding surf was all that Janis could hear; it matched the beating of her heart. Now more than ever, she must act calm, keeping her wits about her.

"Please don't be so suspicious, Floyd. There is nothing between Clifford Green and myself. And I certainly haven't found time while I've been at Winter House to meet anyone."

His grip on her arm tightened. "Don't tell me that. Who was that I saw you with in the rain forest? It certainly wasn't Clifford Green. Who was that man?"

"That was Tim Roark. He's a next-door neighbor. He asked me to come with him to the rain forest. There's a forest scene in the Elyse story. I thought it would give me some idea for the book."

Floyd came to an abrupt stop. He turned to face Janis. "Is that all he is, just a neighbor?"

"Of course. He comes to Winter House quite regularly, mostly to see a Dolores Webster. Dolores Webster and he are very good friends," Janis said, hoping that would reduce Floyd's suspicions.

"Doesn't he work?"

"Yes. He's an architect. But he's independently wealthy so he can pick and choose his assignments."

A slight snarl came from Floyd's lips. "One of those rich playboys, huh? If I were you, I wouldn't have anything more to do with him. You're just not in his league, Janis."

The terror that Janis had experienced when Floyd had first confronted her was beginning to leave. She was beginning to feel merely the old irritation that she had experienced around Floyd of late.

"I don't think it's any of your business who I see, Floyd Phillips! You should not have followed me from New York. And I won't have you telling me who I can see and who I can't."

For a moment Floyd was taken off guard by what Janis had said. Even though he stepped back, he did not release his grip on her arm.

"I have every right to tell you who you can see and who you can't," Floyd said, and there was a smoldering anger in his voice. "You're my girl. Nobody's going to take you away from me."

Janis's mind was whirling. She had to think of something to get Floyd off that precise subject.

"Did you put that cassette tape in my room? And the tape recorder?" she said.

"What tape are you talking about?"

"I think you know very well what tape I'm referring to. The one that told me to leave Winter House. And did you climb into my window and take it away?"

Floyd looked genuinely surprised. "Of course, I didn't do any of those things. I think you're just making all that up."

"I am not making it up," she said. "And I think you were the one who put that tape in my room. Just to scare me into leaving Winter House." Despite her words, she half believed him.

"Even though I didn't do it, it's still a good idea," Floyd said. "I think you should leave Winter House and Oregon."

"How many times do I have to tell you I'm not going to leave here until the illustrations are finished."

"That book," Floyd said with disgust. "Always another book. I'm sick of hearing about those books of yours. There isn't any reason why you should be working. If you were married, you wouldn't have to be working so hard."

"Floyd, how many times do I have to tell you I like

what I'm doing! And as for marriage, that's way in the future. If I ever get married, that is."

Below them Janis could hear the roar of the ocean waves as they crashed against the shoreline. It might have just been her imagination, but the sound of the surf seemed to grow louder and more intense the longer she and Floyd stood at the edge of the cliff.

"You don't know what you're saying, Janis. I want to marry you. Can't you hear what I'm saying?"

"This isn't the time or the place to discuss that, Floyd. Why don't we go back to the house?"

"Back to that group of phonies?" Floyd spat the words out. "I heard enough of their phony talk."

For once Janis had to agree with Floyd, but she didn't want him to know how she felt. There was no telling what he might say to Dolores's guests if he went back to Winter House. Still, she had to think of something to get the two of them away from the edge of the cliff. Floyd might be quite capable of violence in his present state of mind.

"I'm not going back there, and neither are you," he said.

Before Janis knew it, they were struggling at the edge of the cliff. She could feel Floyd's strength as he twisted her body back and forth. Then from somewhere she could hear the sound of hurried footsteps, and a fist shot out from nowhere, hitting Floyd on the chin.

Floyd released Janis's arm and she pivoted to see Tim Roark standing beside her.

"What do you think you're doing?" Tim snapped at Floyd. "Leave Janis alone."

Floyd had recovered from the blow he had received and he started to advance toward Tim, but Tim moved his huge body toward his opponent and Floyd stopped in his tracks.

"This isn't any concern of yours," Floyd said.

"I think it is," was Tim's hard, level reply. "I've followed you here and I don't like the way you're treating Janis."

Janis looked from Tim to Floyd. All the fight had gone out of Floyd, and she could see that his shoulders were sagging.

"I know who you are," Floyd told Tim. "You were with Janis in the rain forest. She said you were just a neighbor."

"A neighbor who cares," Tim replied. "Janis has told me all about you."

Floyd asked Tim, "Just what has she told you?"

"Enough for me to know that you're not wanted around here. I would suggest that you get off this property and go back to New York City. If you know what's good for you, you'll stop bothering Janis."

"And if I don't?" Floyd said.

Tim was silent for a moment. When he spoke, there was a warning tone to his voice. "I think you'd better do what I said."

Floyd hesitated for a moment or two, as though he were trying to decide something. Then he brushed past Janis and Tim and began taking long strides up the pathway.

When he had gone, Tim turned to Janis and said, "I don't think he'll be bothering you again."

Janis stared at the retreating figure of Floyd Phillips. "I wonder."

CHAPTER FOURTEEN

"How did you know we were out here?" Janis asked. Then she remembered that Tim had said he had followed them. "I mean, what brought you outside the house?"

"I missed you. Even with all the noise and chattering, I felt that something was missing," Tim said.

"So you came looking for me."

He shrugged. "It was only natural, wasn't it? If you weren't at the party, you either had to be in your room or outside. That wasn't very hard to figure out."

Suddenly, Tim seemed different to Janis. His voice sounded different. Gone was the concern he had shown when Floyd was there. Had it just been a pretense on his part to make her believe that he was actually concerned about her? Janis was bewildered and confused by this sudden shift in Tim's personality.

"Whatever brought you here, I'm thankful," Janis said.

"Are you all right?" Tim said, sounding concerned again. "He didn't hurt you, did he?"

"Just a little bit shook up. He frightened me more than anything. Floyd was always a possessive and jealous person, but I never thought he was quite so obsessed."

"Then he did hurt you?"

Janis shook her head. "It was just his attitude and his anger. At this point I almost think he's capable of anything."

"What did he tell you while you two were out here?"

"Not very much. He just kept saying I shouldn't be living here at Winter House. That I didn't belong here. He kept insisting that I return to New York City. And he wanted me to give up my work."

Tim gently took Janis's arm and started leading her back to the house.

"Maybe that wouldn't be such a bad idea," he said.

Janis said, "What are you saying? I can't give up my work! I like what I'm doing. And regardless of what you or Floyd Phillips or anyone else at Winter House thinks, I'm not leaving until I finish the sketches."

Tim glanced down at Janis. In the moonlight she could see he was frowning. But she could not tell if that frown was from anger or concern.

Tim said, "You are a stubborn one, aren't you? What did Floyd have in mind when he asked you to come back to New York City? Marriage?"

Janis hesitated. She wondered just how much she should confide in him.

"That did come up," Janis said. "Among other things."

"What other things?"

"I asked him about the tape that I found in my room when I first arrived."

For a second Tim's grip on her arm tightened. It was almost imperceptible, but Janis had noticed it.

"What did he say?"

"He denied putting it in my room. And he denied coming back for it," Janis said.

"It's only natural that he would deny it when you confronted him with it."

Janis was not that certain. "I don't know. But somehow I believe Floyd about that. I've known him for quite a while. He does some dumb, impulsive things. But he isn't a liar. Now that I think about it, I believe he didn't put the tape in my room. He always admits to the things he does. Always."

"And did you believe him when he asked you to marry him?" Tim asked.

"Yes, I did. This isn't the first time he's broached the question."

"I see," Tim said. "And may I ask what your answer was to his proposal."

"I made it very clear to him that marriage was out of the question for me right now."

"Marriage to Floyd, you mean," Tim said.

"I mean marriage, period," Janis said with finality.

"I see," Tim said, quickening his stride. "But Floyd isn't the only man in the world. When the right one comes along, you'll change your mind."

"I hope you're right."

Tim chuckled. "At least you're beginning to show

a little optimism. We'd better get back to the party. They'll be beginning to wonder what happened to us. Not that I really care."

"You're not having a good time?"

"With that group of people? I've seen their kind before. All the money in the world, but they're a very bored, lonely bunch of people."

So Tim felt the same way she did in regard to Dolores's friends. Tim obviously had money himself, but he did not feel at ease with these people. Maybe it was because he still occupied himself with worthwhile projects. But did he? Janis only had his word for that. However, Tim did not strike her as someone belonging to that group inside the house.

"I thought I was the only one who had those ideas about the people in there," Janis said.

"I don't trust the lot of them. They are about as phony as you can get. Why Dolores puts up with them, I'll never know."

Janis said nothing for a moment. She tried to think that Dolores was not like the rest of her guests, but in her heart Janis knew better.

They paused when they arrived at the house, and Tim turned to Janis, saying, "You go on inside. I want to have a look around just to make certain that Floyd Phillips has really gone."

What Tim said gave Janis a momentary feeling of panic. "You don't suppose he is still around, do you? That he hasn't left the property?"

"From all you've told me of him, I wouldn't put it past him to be hiding someplace. He was just too willing to give up and walk away back there on the cliff."

Janis could not refrain from glancing furtively into

the darkness that surrounded the house. If Floyd was still out there, he was probably watching the two of them at this very moment. She did not want Floyd to resort to any violence that would injure anyone. And yet, surprisingly, she cared enough for him as a friend not to wish any harm to come to him.

"Maybe I should go with you," Janis said. "Somehow I feel responsible for his being here."

Tim made a guttural sound with his husky voice. "Don't be foolish. It was not your fault that Floyd followed you from New York. If what you told me was the truth, you never gave him any encouragement to come here to Oregon."

"It was the truth. I made it perfectly clear to Floyd how I felt towards him. He just would not listen to what I was telling him."

"All I can say is that either he didn't hear you or you weren't emphatic enough when you spoke to him," Tim said, and that rankled Janis.

"You're entitled to believe whatever you choose," she said. "The fact remains that Floyd did follow me and he's here in Oregon now."

"And you had better go inside," Tim said in a half-teasing tone of voice. "I won't be long. I'll just take a walk around the premises and be sure that he has really gone away."

"Please be careful, Tim," Janis said as he released his hold on her arm.

"Thanks for the concern. But don't you worry. I can take care of myself and Floyd Phillips too," Tim said, then walked away slowly.

Janis stood there for a few moments, thinking about Tim and Floyd. She said a silent prayer that Tim would not be harmed. And she wanted Floyd not to be on the grounds. She hoped he had left for good.

The sound of laughter brought Janis out of her reverie and she reluctantly walked toward the French doors that led into the living room. Once inside, she looked around and came to the realization that she had not even been missed.

Janis walked among the throng of people who were polite but distant. She knew that she would never fit into their life-style. And she really did not care. Looking around, she saw the smug almost spiteful looks on the guests' faces and she longed for the evening to come to an end.

"You look lost, little child," said a voice from her left, and she turned to see a man in his late thirties standing there. "Come with me and I'll get you a drink of punch."

Janis was about to refuse, but she saw that the man was a trifle intoxicated and she was afraid he might create a scene if she did not comply with his wishes.

The man put his arm around her waist and Janis instinctively tensed at his touch. But he did not sense the change in her.

When they got to the punch bowl, he filled a glass for her and ceremoniously handed it to her. "I didn't get your name. I'm Bradley Graves."

"Janis Long," she said and pretended to take a sip from the glass.

"What group did you come with?" Bradley said as he made a sweeping gesture with one arm.

"No group. I live here. Or rather I'm staying here as a guest."

"Ah, yes. Now I remember. You're the artist that

dear Dolores was telling me about."

The way Bradley said Dolores's name, Janis could tell that he had little use for his hostess.

"I'm an illustrator," Janis corrected him.

"An illustrator? What do you illustrate?" Bradley's voice had risen somewhat.

"Books," Janis said. "Children's books. I do the Elyse series. I don't know whether you've heard of them or not."

"Everyone has heard of the Elyse series. To tell you the truth, I enjoy them very much. But then I'm not one for an intellectual challenge."

Janis smiled and said, "I'm pleased that you've read them. I guess somebody helped you with all the hard words."

Instead of being insulted, Bradley Graves burst out in laughter. "Touche, my dear. Touche. I deserved that," he said, then refilled his glass from the punch bowl. "With a little bit of practice, I think you would fit in very nicely with this crowd."

I certainly hope not, Janis said to herself. But she just smiled at Bradley in the most pleasant manner she could muster.

"Ah, there is our hostess now," he said with another sweep of his hand. "What a colossal bore she is. If it wasn't for the fact that Dolores was so beautiful, nobody would have anything to do with her."

What terrible people these are, Janis thought to herself. They are such hypocrites. Here they come to a party given by someone they can't stand. Suddenly, Janis wished that the party was over, that she could be safe in her room, away from all these phony people.

"Look at her now, on the prowl," Bradley said.

"She's looking for that architect friend of hers, I bet. Dolores has her eyes on him. And whatever Dolores wants, she usually winds up getting. The poor guy won't stand a chance."

"Excuse me, please," Janis said, wanting to get as far away as possible from this man.

It was bad enough to know how Dolores felt about Tim. Janis didn't need to be reminded of it.

In her rush to get away from Bradley, Janis bumped into Lucas Green, who was standing at the edge of the crowd.

"Sorry," Janis said to Lucas.

"That's all right. Just an occupational hazard. These parties of Dolores's. I don't know why I bothered to even come down."

So even Lucas was not enjoying himself.

Suddenly, he asked, "Where have you been? I watched you leave a while back. And then I saw Tim go out the same door. You two don't have something cooking, do you? Dolores won't like that." There was a touch of malice in his voice.

"It wasn't like that at all. I needed a breath of fresh air and I went outside. There was somebody else outside and Tim came to my rescue."

Lucas focused his eyes intently on Janis. They were studying her with a look that she could not understand. "What are you saying?" he asked.

Since Janis had gone this far, she decided to tell Lucas everything. She told him all about Floyd, how they had met, what had developed between them. Then she told Lucas about what had happened in the rain forest and now, lastly, what had happened on the cliff.

Lucas had listened with mounting curiosity to Janis's

words. She got an uncomfortable feeling that his mind was racing inside his skull. For a moment while she had been talking, she saw his eyes narrow into tiny slits, and a deep frown crept across his forehead. But then his eyes opened and the frown lines vanished.

"Well, I hope we've seen the last of this Floyd whatever-his-name-is. We certainly don't need someone prowling around the grounds. I'm sure my father wouldn't approve of that."

"I'm sure he's gone by this time. But he did tell me in no uncertain terms that I shouldn't be staying here at Winter House."

"Maybe he's right," Lucas said. "Maybe you should go back to New York. It doesn't look as though Oregon agrees with you."

With that Lucas walked away.

Glancing around aimlessly, Janis saw Dolores walking toward the French doors. Then Janis saw Tim Roark enter and look around.

Dolores moved toward Tim and they both began to talk. Then Dolores slipped an arm through Tim's and guided him across the room. The words of Bradley Graves came back to haunt Janis as she watched the two of them together.

CHAPTER FIFTEEN

By the time the party was over, Janis was weary and ready to go to bed. But she found herself tossing and turning, her thoughts on Tim Roark. She just could not figure the man out. Sometimes he appeared to be very attentive towards her and then at other times it was as though he withdrew into a cold, chilly shell. And then there was Dolores. Janis had known, of course, that Dolores had set her cap for Tim and she was ruthless enough to get whatever she wanted. But how did she, Janis, really feel toward Tim? All she knew was that when he was around she got a warm, pleasant feeling in the pit of her stomach. A feeling that was not there when she had gone out with Floyd Phillips.

Had Floyd lied to her when she had confronted him with the tape that she had found in her room when she first arrived at Winter House? Was he the person who had shoved her on the steps? Had he entered her room to remove the tape and the recorder?

He had readily admitted that he had watched her through the dining-room window. So it just had to be Floyd who had done all these other things to her. Still, in the back of her mind, she couldn't bring herself to believe that Floyd would do these things. As she had told Tim, Floyd had never been a liar.

If it hadn't been Floyd, then who could it have been? Tim Roark apparently had easy access to the house and he could have planted the tape in her room long before she arrived at the house. And he was in the house that night when there was a brief power failure. Yes, it could have been Tim. Only, Janis could not figure out why he had done these things, if he were guilty.

There were three other possibilities if Tim was not guilty. It could have been Jonas, the gardener, for one. He certainly was a disagreeable person and he certainly did not care for her. Anyway, that was the impression he had made on her the night she had arrived. Jonas knew the house and grounds as well as anybody connected with the place. Yet, there again, what motive would he have?

For that matter, what might the motive be for Lucas Green? Even though Janis had been at Winter House for some time, she just hadn't been able to get close to Clifford Green's only offspring. Lucas was hospitable, but there it all ended. It was as though he wore a mask that he did not want anyone to penetrate. Janis suddenly thought that this was all wild speculation on her part, and she turned on her side.

She did not want to go to sleep with Dolores on her mind, so she thought about the book illustrations. That

seemed to calm Janis down, but she found that, before
sleep came, she had once again let her thoughts drift
back to Tim Roark.

When she finally did close her eyes, she had dis-
turbing and frightening dreams. At one point she found
herself struggling for her life at the edge of the cliff
overlooking the sea. Below her, she could see the
pounding, treacherous surf.

Someone was trying to push her over the cliff and
she fought with all her strength to save herself. Time
and again she tried to see who was doing this to her,
but a cloud covered the moon and she could not make
out who it was.

When Janis awoke the next morning, she felt as
though she had not slept a wink. She took a cold,
bracing shower and that brought her fully awake. After
she had put on a pair of burnt-orange slacks and a beige
sweater, she was beginning to feel like her old self
once again.

Janis sat before the mirror and brushed her wheat-
colored hair until it crackled. Then she applied a glossy
lipstick and studied her face for a moment. In spite of
everything that had been happening to her since she
had arrived at Winter House, she seemed to look all
right. She was certainly no match for Dolores, but she
was not dismayed by her appearance.

Breakfast was a quiet meal. Dolores and Lucas did
most of the talking and Janis got the impression that
they were speaking as though she were not present in
the room. This might have bothered her at any other
time but not today. She welcomed the lack of attention
she was receiving. She could concentrate on what she
had to do that day. She knew from the past that the

creative urge was upon her. All the walking about in the halls and rooms of Winter House and the studying she had done was over. Now she had to get her impressions down on paper. Little Elyse's new adventure demanded to be brought to life.

"What do you think, Miss Long?" Dolores's voice cut through her musings.

"I'm sorry," Janis said. "I'm afraid I wasn't listening."

"It doesn't matter," Dolores said with a deep sigh of disgust. "You were probably out there somewhere with all those weird things you illustrate in your books."

"That's enough, Dolores," Lucas said, and Dolores shot him a very cold, hard look. "We were just discussing what you told me last night. Do you remember?"

Janis had to think for a moment. Last night seemed eons ago. "You mean about Floyd Phillips?"

"Was that his name?" Lucas said.

"That's right. What about Floyd?"

"Nothing, really," Lucas said. "Unless he comes back to the house. In that case, maybe we should tell the authorities. I doubt that my father would appreciate someone like Floyd Phillips roaming about the premises."

The tone of Lucas's voice irritated Janis. It was true that Floyd had been prowling on private property and he obviously was somewhat disturbed, but it was the attitude of Lucas that bothered her.

"I don't think he'll be back. Tim put him on the run last night. Floyd is not really a dangerous person."

"That's what you say," Dolores said and then took a sip of coffee. "Frankly, the man sounds as though he might be dangerous. You certainly do pick the strangest people for friends."

Before Janis could stop herself, she said, "I could say the same for you, Dolores."

Dolores's eyes narrowed into tiny slits. But Janis did not care. She was tired of Dolores's cutting remarks and she did not intend to put up with them any longer.

"I suppose that includes Tim Roark?" Dolores said, glaring at Janis. "After all, he is a friend of mine."

"So you would like to believe," Janis said, meeting Dolores's intense stare.

"You had better watch your step, Miss Long," Dolores said. "That's a warning."

Lucas leaned across the table. "Come now, Dolores. After all, Father has given orders that Miss Long's every wish is to be granted. She has the deciding voice here at Winter House."

Janis switched her attention from Dolores to Lucas. She studied his face for an instant, but it was inscrutable. Whatever his private thoughts about her were, he certainly wasn't revealing them by his outward appearance.

"I'm just a guest here. Just as Dolores is a guest. As soon as my work is finished, I will be leaving."

"How is your work going?" Lucas asked.

"Very well. I intend to spend the entire day working. The sooner I get the illustrations finished, the better. Then I'll be on my way home."

"I'm sure that will please my father," Lucas said in a low tone of voice.

"He has a lot of faith in me. And I intend not to shatter that faith. I happen to think very highly of your father."

"That's admirable," Dolores said and then she turned to face Lucas.

She immediately began to once again discuss the party, deliberately excluding Janis from the conversation. Janis finished her coffee and walked out of the room.

When she was in the hallway, she paused for a moment and breathed a deep sigh of relief. She heard a movement from her right and turned to see Mary Lee standing there with some towels draped over one arm.

"Don't let them get you down, Janis," Mary Lee said with a friendliness that touched Janis's heart.

Of all the people at Winter House, she liked the pretty young daughter of Winnifred the best.

"Oh, they aren't, really. I guess I just don't understand either one of them."

"I know it's none of my business, but Miss Webster can be quite a handful when she wants to be. And Mr. Green really needs to be working more. It would give him something to occupy his time and mind."

Janis smiled at Mary Lee knowing that the girl really did not mean to gossip. "Just what does Lucas do for a living anyway?"

Mary Lee thought for a moment and then said, "I'm not really sure. He goes away sometimes for hours. Where I don't know. But I'm certain he must work. He does have expensive tastes in clothes, and that luxury car of his must have cost a fortune."

After that Janis went upstairs and got to work. She studied the sketches she had done and decided that they weren't half bad. She got out the manuscript and curled up on the bed to reread it for the umpteenth time. Certain passages fairly cried out for illustrations and she made a mark opposite them.

Finally, she got up and walked over to her desk. For about three hours she lost herself in her work. The creative spark in her had fanned itself to a full flame.

After a very productive morning, Janis sat back and idly massaged her neck. She had been sitting in one position for such a long time that a slight cramp had taken hold of her. She stretched and the discomfort soon left her.

Janis decided that she needed a break. A cup of coffee would certainly taste good right about now.

Leaving her room, she felt those prying eyes following her every movement. Then she shrugged off the feeling and hurried down to the kitchen.

Winnifred poured her a cup of coffee and Janis took it upstairs. She was surprised to see Jonas standing outside her room staring at her door. He must have sensed her presence because he turned and the expression on his face was one of guilt.

"What are you doing up here, Jonas?" Janis asked the gardener.

Jonas hesitated, then said, "Winnifred asked me to fetch something for her."

"From my room?"

"It wasn't in your room," Jonas said defensively.

"Did you find what you were looking for?" Janis asked needlessly since Jonas had nothing in his hands.

"No, I didn't. Winnifred must have been mistaken," he said as he brushed past her and went clomping down the stairs.

Janis opened the door to her room and went inside. A quick glance assured her that everything was just as she had left it.

"I'm getting jumpy," she said. "Maybe this coffee will help quiet my nerves."

Sitting down at her desk, Janis slowly sipped the coffee. She began to think about Jonas and what he was really doing up here. The story he had told her did not ring true and she began to wonder if he had been the one who had left the tape in her room and done all the other things. Yet she could find no motive for him.

After lunch, Janis again worked on the illustrations. Everything else seemed to be out of her mind when she was working. And she welcomed this opportunity to forget all about her problems. All about Tim Roark and Floyd Phillips, the hateful Dolores Webster, and the enigmatic Lucas Green. And Jonas. She was so involved in her work that she almost jumped when there was a rap on her door.

"Who is it?" she called out.

"Mary Lee. There's a call for you. Do you want to take it in the library?"

"I'll be right down," Janis said.

Her caller turned out to be Floyd Phillips.

"Janis," he said, "please don't hang up on me. Although you have every right to."

"What do you want, Floyd?" Janis tried to keep her voice even and emotionless.

"I just want to talk to you, Jan. Just for a little while. Would that be possible?"

There was something different in Floyd's voice. It did not sound the way it had last night. He sounded more reasonable and also contrite.

"Floyd, I really don't think I should—"

"Listen, Jan, please listen to me. I'm leaving here

in a few hours. Going back to New York. And I just couldn't go until I've explained some things to you. I know I don't deserve it and I won't hold it against you if you refuse to see me, but could you?"

Somehow Janis felt a wave of sympathy for Floyd. After all, he had been her friend, and it wasn't his fault that he had been overwhelmed by a one-sided infatuation.

"Where are you?"

Floyd's voice suddenly sounded encouraged. "At a restaurant in town. It's called the Sandpiper. Will you come?"

Janis hesitated for a moment or two and then she sighed and said, "Yes, Floyd. I'll be there as soon as I can."

When Janis hung up, she found that even though Floyd sounded different, she could not get rid of the uneasiness she felt.

CHAPTER SIXTEEN

After Janis had hung up, she stared at the telephone, wondering if she had done the right thing. Perhaps this was a trick of Floyd's to get her alone. But they wouldn't be alone. He wanted to meet her in a public place with people around.

At that moment Janis felt that she was not alone right now. She turned and saw Tim standing in the doorway.

"You were deep in thought," he said. "Is anything the matter?"

"I just got a phone call. A phone call from Floyd," Janis said softly.

Tim asked, "What did he want?"

"He wants to talk to me," Janis said.

Tim said, "Talk to you! He's got some nerve."

"I don't know. Floyd sounded different. Like maybe he's changed."

"Don't let him fool you. I doubt that he's changed. He's just using a different tactic."

Janis shook her head. "I don't think so. There was something in his voice, something that I can't explain. Anyway, I've got to give him a chance."

Tim advanced a few steps into the room. "You aren't serious. Not after what happened to you last night."

"I know it sounds crazy. But, Tim, you didn't hear his voice," Janis said, trying to make Tim understand what she felt toward Floyd.

"Come on, Janis. Face facts. The guy has a problem, he's not rational. And someone in his position is probably very sly and crafty."

"Maybe you are right," Janis said thoughtfully. "And then again maybe you aren't. At any rate, I've got to take a chance and believe that he's telling me the truth. After all, Tim, I have known him for a long time. We were friends. I do owe him that much."

Tim shook his head. "You don't owe him a thing, Janis. But I can see by the look on your face that you're determined to see him."

"I'm afraid I have to," Janis replied in a quiet voice.

"Where are you meeting him?" Tim asked.

"At the Sandpiper. He told me that he's leaving Oregon in a few hours and that he wanted to see me before he went back to New York City. It's not much that he's asking."

"Personally, I think he's asking a great deal. And I really am concerned about you going there."

"Why? He wouldn't try anything in a restaurant."

"Wouldn't he? You yourself told me of the scenes he made when you went out with him in New York.

What makes you think it will be any different this
time?"

Janis didn't reply for a moment. She let Tim's words
sink in. She carefully weighed what he had said against
what Floyd had told her on the phone.

Then she said, "It's hard to explain, Tim. But I don't
think Floyd is the same man that he was a few hours
ago. Besides, the worst thing he ever actually did was
make a scene. I don't think he'd even do that anymore.
Call it woman's intuition or whatever you will. In some
crazy way I believe that he's telling me the truth."

"Do you totally believe that?"

Janis remembered the uneasiness that had struck her
when she had hung up after Floyd's call. She pushed
that feeling away and clung to what she presently believed to be the truth.

"For a while I was doubtful. But not anymore."

Tim sighed deeply. "Very well if you are determined
to go. I'll follow you just to make sure that nothing
happens to you."

Janis quickly shook her head. "Don't, Tim. If Floyd
sees you, it might ruin everything. That jealous nature
of his might flare up again."

"You can't expect me to just sit around here doing
nothing while you might be in danger," Tim said and
there was real concern in his voice.

"I won't be in danger. It's not going to be like that
at all. We're just going to talk. Then I'm coming right
back here to Winter House."

Janis studied Tim's face which displayed in no uncertain terms his concern for her. Yet she couldn't
totally rely on what she saw in Tim's face. He had

fooled her in the past. Janis still did not know how deep Tim's feelings were for Dolores.

"I guess there's no stopping you," Tim said. "Apparently, you've made up your mind."

"Yes, I have."

"May I ask you something, Janis? And I'd like to have an honest answer."

Janis's eyebrows rose. "I've always tried to be honest. Just what is your question?"

"Have you told me the truth about Floyd? By that I mean the way you feel about him?"

"Of course. There's nothing romantic between us. There never has been. Anyway, not as far as I'm concerned. All I ever wanted from him was friendship. That was the way it was at the beginning, but then Floyd changed. Now I'm not even sure that I think of him as a friend. Is that what you wanted to know?"

Tim appeared to relax. A faint, ironic smile touched his lips. "I just had to be sure. After all, the guy comes all the way from New York to Oregon. I just assumed you must have given him a little encouragement to go to that extreme."

Janis wasn't certain whether she was angry at Tim's remark or not. "There was not any encouragement on my part. You can take my word for that."

"Okay, I'll take your word for that. It was just something that was bothering me. You know, you are a very attractive woman, Janis. I could see where it would be easy for a man to misunderstand your intentions."

Janis was becoming tired of the conversation and she decided to change the subject. "I'd better be on my way. I told Floyd I would be there in a little while."

"Okay. But are you sure you don't want me to follow

along? I wouldn't have to go into the Sandpiper. I could just stay in my car. Just in case things didn't work out the way you think they will."

"I would rather you didn't, Tim. But I do thank you for your concern and caring."

"Oh, Tim is very concerned about people. And quite caring too," said a feminine voice from the doorway, and Janis shifted her attention from Tim to Dolores.

The statuesque beauty cast a disdainful look at Janis and then became all sweetness and light when Tim turned to look at her.

"Hello, Dolores. I didn't know you were standing there," he said in a low voice.

"I was standing here just long enough to not understand anything that's going on. But I gather it has something to do with this Floyd character that Lucas was telling me about."

Even though Janis was disappointed in Floyd Phillips, she did not appreciate the way Dolores was talking about him.

"Janis received a call from Floyd. He asked to meet her at the Sandpiper," Tim said, and Janis almost wished that he had said nothing.

"Good idea," Dolores said. "And while she's with Floyd, I'd like to talk to you, Tim. There were so many people at the party last night I hardly had a chance to say anything to you in private."

"It was your party and your friends," Tim said in an amused tone of voice.

For a split second the carefully controlled mask on Dolores's face slipped and she looked like a misunderstood waif. Then, as quickly as the mask had slipped, Dolores put it back on again.

She sidled up to Tim and said, "If it were anyone else making that statement, I might be peeved. Somehow, coming from you, I'm not upset. You just have a way with words, Tim."

That was too much for Janis to take. "If you will excuse me, I'll be going."

Before Janis left, she couldn't help but notice the look on Tim's face. It was almost as though he were pleading with her not to leave him alone with Dolores. But Janis didn't let that bother her. Tim obviously liked Dolores's attention or he wouldn't put up with it.

Janis hurried out of the room and up the stairs. She got her purse, making certain the keys to the car were in it, and then hurried back downstairs once again. She heard Tim and Dolores talking as she rushed outside to her car.

Once Janis reached Call's Bay, it didn't take her long to find the Sandpiper. It was the only big restaurant in the small town. Janis maneuvered the car into the parking lot and got out.

As she opened the restaurant door, she saw Floyd standing in the vestibule. She automatically paused and then she saw him smile at her. Floyd walked towards her and stretched out his hand for her to shake.

"I'm glad you came, Jan. Let's go inside. I have a table waiting for us," Floyd said in the same tone of voice he had used over the telephone.

Floyd did not take her arm or touch her in any way as they walked the length of the dining room to the table he had secured for them.

After they had been seated, he said, "Would you care for anything? Some dinner or whatever?"

"Coffee and a chef's salad would be fine," Janis said.

Floyd gave the waitress their order and then he leaned back in his chair. "Like I said, I'm glad you came, Janis."

"Just what was it that you wanted to see me about, Floyd? You sounded urgent and pleading on the telephone," Janis said in a gentle tone of voice.

Floyd studied her face for a moment and then said, "I guess what I want to say more than anything else is that I'm sorry for the way I have been behaving toward you, Jan. Last night I was awake until about three o'clock thinking about the way I've been acting. It was like I was watching a motion picture of my life these past few months and I didn't like what I saw."

Janis listened quietly, not wanting to display the anxiety she was secretly feeling.

"I don't know what caused me to be the way I was— no, that's not true, I do. It was childishness, Jan, plain and simple. But I think I'm over that now. Adults should realize they can't always have the one they love. That's life. I'm not asking you to like me, Jan, but maybe in time we might be friends. Believe me, I won't bother you again. Not here in Oregon or back in New York City. I'm finally growing up. I hope you believe what I'm saying."

Looking into Floyd's eyes, Janis could see how painful all this was for him and she could tell that he was speaking the truth from his heart.

"Somehow I believe you, Floyd. And I know it took a lot of courage for you to say these things to me."

Floyd gave a deep sigh of relief. "You know, I feel

like a ton of bricks has been removed from my shoulders. Every once in a while when I was in that hiding place at Winter House I started to feel I was acting like a big baby."

"A hiding place? Where is that?" Janis asked.

"I thought you knew about that. I found it by accident. It's built into the side of the cliff. Right below that tall hemlock tree with the twisted branches. You'd never find it if you didn't know it was there. The entrance is hidden by some rocks, but I slipped past them."

"This hiding place, what's it like? Probably abandoned and full of dust. Spiderwebs all over the place?"

Floyd shook his head. "No, it's nothing like that. It's been used and recently. It's more of a workshop than a hiding place. There are all sorts of tools lying around and some furniture. They look like antiques to me, but I don't know anything about antiques."

"How odd," Janis said and idly wondered who might be using the place.

Maybe she could use it in the Elyse book. She would check on it when she got back to Winter House.

"Anyway, now you know why I called you and asked you to meet me here. I just couldn't go away thinking that you disliked me, Jan."

Suddenly, Janis knew that she didn't dislike Floyd, not in the least. And she told him as much.

"I hope that your illustrations turn out just great," Floyd said. "And that you continue to work for Clifford Green. You know, I'm not even jealous of him any longer. What a relief that is."

After that their food came, and they chatted for a while longer. Then Janis stood up to go. She shook hands with Floyd and left him at the table. She felt very good as she saw him sitting there before she left the restaurant.

CHAPTER SEVENTEEN

By the time Janis reached Winter House her good mood had vanished. Now she was absolutely certain Floyd had not left the tape in her room or tried to push her down the stairs. So who had done those things? And why?

With a sigh, she got out of the car and walked toward the house. It had grown dark and the moon shone brightly in an unclouded sky.

Yes, she thought, there was a certain beauty about the Oregon countryside even at night. She would miss all this when she finished the book and had to return to New York.

Thinking these things brought a heavy lump to her throat. She knew that she would miss Tim Roark once she had left Winter House. What were her true feelings toward the handsome architect? How deep were they?

Oh, well, he probably didn't care that much about her. So she might as well grow up, the way Floyd was doing.

Janis paused before going inside the house. Even though it was a beautiful home and the furniture priceless, there was a certain aura of foreboding about the place that seemed to wrap its arms around her like some unseen entity. In a way she would be happy to finish her work and leave it.

The rest of the evening Janis roamed restlessly about Winter House studying the place, storing away in her mind what could be used in her drawings. Dolores appeared to deliberately avoid her and those times when they did come into contact the statuesque beauty was cool and detached.

Lucas seemed to be watching Janis although he was not obvious about it. She couldn't help thinking of Mary Lee's words about his expensive tastes. He must be working at something, for there were times when he disappeared from the house for hours.

Once she had noticed that there was a stain on his hands, as though he were working with varnish or shellac. But since Lucas did not volunteer any information, she did not question him. After all, she was just a guest in the house.

By the time it was ten-thirty, Janis found herself yawning and went quietly up the stairs to her room. A fierce wind had arisen and it moaned around the eaves of the house. Janis closed her door and got ready for bed. She was not in the mood to read, so she slipped between the covers and turned out the lamp on the nightstand.

Lying in the dark, she listened to the sound of the

wind and drew the covers up to her chin. She said a
quick prayer that Floyd would have a safe journey back
to New York. In her heart Janis wanted the best for
Floyd. She hoped that what he had told her at the
Sandpiper was true, that he had finally come to a form
of peace within himself. Janis always wanted people
to be happy. And maybe Floyd would finally find the
right girl for himself when he returned to New York.

The wind stopped for a brief time and Janis became
aware of footsteps in the corridor. The hallway was
not fully carpeted, but there were several throw rugs
scattered about. As she listened, the footsteps seemed
to come closer to her door. Then there was a pause
and Janis knew that someone was standing outside her
room.

Tossing the covers aside, she got out of bed and
walked across the room. Because it was so dark, she
did not see the chair that she had pulled back from the
desk earlier, and she tripped over it, hurting her bare
toes. She gave a sharp cry of pain. Then, limping to
the door, she opened it, but there was no one in the
corridor.

She walked out of the room and peered down the
hallway. All she could see were the antiques that were
bathed in the light from the wall sconces.

Janis stood in the corridor for a while, waiting to
see if the person who had stood in front of her door
would make an appearance. Then she turned and went
back into her room.

Avoiding the desk chair, she hurried back to the
comfort and safety of her bed. Who could it have been?
Was it Dolores who had crept down the corridor and

stood before her door? What would she have in mind? Was it just another trick to frighten her into leaving Winter House? Even though Janis had not seen anyone in the corridor, she knew that she hadn't been mistaken. Someone had definitely been out there.

Turning on her side, she thought about Lucas. He would have had time to rush back to his room after she had cried out. There had been enough time for that. Or maybe it wasn't either Dolores or Lucas. Maybe it had been Jonas. Janis could still remember how she had caught him standing before her room when she had reached the landing on the stairs.

Yes, Jonas was a very good candidate. Yet she could not understand why the gardener would wish to frighten her. She had never done anything to him. What possible reason could Jonas have for resenting her?

Or maybe—and Janis did not want to think of this— it could have been Tim Roark. He certainly had free access to the house. It was all so bewildering. And she had been foolish enough to once think that when Floyd Phillips was caught, all her troubles would be over. It just wasn't to be. Now she was positive that Floyd had had nothing to do with what was going on here at Winter House—aside from the things he had admitted. He was on his way home. And maybe she should go too.

"That's enough of that," Janis murmured. "You came here to illustrate that book. Won't you look foolish when you tell Clifford Green that you were scared away from Winter House!"

She knew that she would never tell Clifford Green that and that she would certainly not be driven away until she got some answers to the questions that were bothering her.

Having temporarily forgotten about the person who had stood outside her door, Janis yawned as her eyelids began to droop. This certainly had been a very unusual day, she thought. She had never imagined she would be hearing the words that Floyd Phillips had said to her at the Sandpiper. She was happy that he was beginning to change and she felt better knowing that he was on his way back to New York.

The last person she thought of was Tim Roark. With a pleasant sigh, Janis drifted off to sleep.

At first Janis's dreams were warm and full of pleasant scenes of rolling hills and dazzling flowers. Then abruptly the dreams changed and she found herself a prisoner in an old abandoned hut. In the distance Janis could hear the dreaded sound of footsteps and she tried frantically to get out of the hut.

Without warning, the door gave way and she found herself standing on the treacherous cliff. Below her she could see the angry surf pounding against the rocks. Then Janis felt hands on her back forcing her to move to the edge. She tried to fight, to shrug off the hands, but she seemed frail and weak.

When Janis opened her eyes, she saw with a great feeling of relief that it was daylight and she was still in her comfortable bed. It took her at least twenty minutes to get over the nightmare. It had seemed so real, so lifelike. Then she remembered what Floyd had told her about the place he had been hiding in, and at least that gave her some comfort. Somehow his words had inspired the dream, insinuating their way into her mind and creating the atmosphere of the nightmare.

Dressing in a pair of jeans and a gray velour pullover, Janis went down to breakfast. She did not feel like meeting either Dolores or Lucas, so she walked into the kitchen. Both Winnifred and Mary Lee were sitting at the small table, sipping coffee.

"Miss Long," Winnifred exclaimed. "Is anything the matter?"

Janis shook her head. "Nothing. I just thought I would have breakfast in here this morning. Is that all right? It won't bother you, will it?"

Winnifred got to her feet, her smile wide on her face. "Heavens, no. It's just that it's a little unusual. I'll fix you some eggs and bacon. It won't take a minute."

"Thank you," Janis said as she poured herself a cup of coffee and sat next to Mary Lee.

"Did you enjoy the party the other night, Janis?" Mary Lee asked after taking a quick swallow of the hot, steaming liquid.

"To tell you the truth, I didn't," Janis said. "It just wasn't the sort of thing I enjoy. But I suppose Dolores and her friends had a good time. Something did happen that was interesting, though."

Mary Lee's eyes were wide with interest as Janis began to tell her and Winnifred all about Floyd Phillips. Somehow she did not feel any desire to hold anything back from the two women. She trusted both of them implicitly. When she had finished, Winnifred placed a platter of eggs, buttered toast, and Canadian bacon before her.

"You've been through a lot, poor child," Winnifred

said as she made a clicking sound with her tongue. "Still, I think that man Phillips has learned his lesson and I don't think he'll be bothering you for a while."

"I think you're right," Janis said. "Do you or Mary Lee know anything about a hiding place or a cave anywhere on the property?"

Winnifred looked at Mary Lee and they both shook their heads.

"It's the first I've heard of it," Mary Lee said as she looked from her mother to Janis. "Do you think there really is such a place?"

"Floyd said there was," Janis said. "He told me it was full of old furniture. Antique at that. And that there was sort of a workshop there."

"Sounds strange to me," Winnifred said. And then she went to the cupboard and brought out a book. Walking over to Janis, she said, "Would you mind autographing this last Elyse book, Miss Long? I'm going to give it to one of my grandchildren as a birthday present."

Janis was touched that Winnifred had gone to all that trouble and she wrote something particularly thoughtful on the title page. After that she consumed her breakfast. She and Mary Lee just talked about nothing in particular. Mary Lee was so down-to-earth and easy to talk to that Janis felt her spirits rise after she had finished eating and had left the kitchen. She would miss both Winnifred and Mary Lee when she went back to New York.

Once outside the kitchen, Janis went up the stairs to her room. She gathered up her sketch pad and some pencils, pens, and pastels. Then she headed for the library and did a few drawings of Elyse and some of the other characters, showing them in various parts of the house.

After she had completed those pictures, Janis left the library and walked into the study. She took her sketches and all her art materials with her. The study would play a prominent part in the story. Of course, the room would be altered to better fit the plot.

Glancing about the study, Janis noticed the two chairs with the bears carved in the center of the backs. Janis stared at the two chairs for a moment, feeling a little perplexed. She had thought the bears were facing each other, but now they were both facing in the same direction. Surely, she had been mistaken when she'd thought they were facing each other. It had just been a fanciful notion.

Taking a seat opposite the two chairs, Janis began to sketch them. She was so busy working away that she did not hear Lucas when he came into the room.

"Hard at work, I see," Lucas said, and Janis almost jumped.

"You startled me," Janis said. "I shouldn't be so jumpy."

"What are you sketching?"

Janis did not look at Lucas but gestured with her pencil. "Those two chairs. They have an interesting design in them that I think I can use in the book. But I'll probably have to change the bears to some other animal."

"They don't look all that interesting to me. Why don't you sketch something in the library?" Lucas said in a low tone of voice.

Janis glanced up at him and she saw that he was staring at the chairs with a look that she could only describe as alarm. Then the look disappeared from his face as he turned his attention back to her sketch pad. "However, you are the artist and you know what's best for the book."

With that Lucas walked out of the room. Dolores was just passing and she glanced in at Janis.

Seeing her sketch pad in her hands, Dolores wandered over and looked down at the rough sketch. "You aren't going to use those chairs in your book, I hope."

"I do a lot of background sketches that aren't used in the book," Janis said. "It all depends on what will go best with the text."

"If I were you, I wouldn't bother with those two chairs," Dolores said, then walked out of the room.

Janis stared after the woman for a moment wondering why she had suddenly taken such an interest in her work. Then she shrugged and returned her attention to the two chairs.

Just as she was finishing the sketch, Mary Lee poked her head inside. "Excuse me, Janis, telephone for you. It's Mr. Roark."

"Thanks, Mary Lee. I needed a break," Janis said and hurried to the telephone.

"Hi, Tim," she said when she placed the instrument to her ear.

"Would this starving artist accept a dinner invitation?" Tim said in mock seriousness.

"I've never been known to turn a dinner invitation down," Janis said in the same tone of voice.

"Great. Then I'll pick you up tonight and we'll eat at my place. Have any objections to that?"

"None in the least. I've wanted to get a good look at your home," Janis replied.

"You'll get your wish tonight. I'll pick you up at six. Okay?"

Janis hung up the telephone and she wondered if she had been too hasty in accepting the invitation. Something told her not to go.

CHAPTER EIGHTEEN

The rest of the morning Janis was busy with her sketches. From time to time she wondered about Tim and the invitation for dinner. In one way she was looking forward to seeing the handsome architect and in another she was apprehensive about going to his house. Once or twice she almost decided to call him and cancel the engagement, but each time she thought about doing that, her curiosity was aroused as to what Tim was up to.

At lunchtime she left the sketches in the study and went into the dining room. Dolores and Lucas were there and a light salad was being served by Winnifred. The only smile Janis received was from Winnifred, who appeared happy to see her.

"Thanks again, Miss Long, for the autograph," Winnifred whispered to her as she served Janis her salad.

158

"That will mean a lot to my granddaughter."

"Don't think anything about it," Janis said. "I was happy to do it."

After Winnifred had gone, Dolores stared at Janis from across the table. "You seem to have made a hit with Winnifred. I've never been able to coax that kind of reaction from her."

"What is your secret, Miss Long?" Lucas asked with a touch of sarcasm in his voice.

"I just autographed a book for her granddaughter," Janis said as she took a sip of iced tea.

"It takes so little to please some people," Dolores said with a smirk.

Janis ignored the barb and turned her attention to her food.

The conversation from then on was strained.

When Lucas finished, he got to his feet. "Well, I've got my work to do. I'll see you two at dinner tonight."

Janis glanced up. "I won't be at dinner tonight. Tim wants me to have dinner at his place."

Lucas shrugged and walked out of the room. Janis looked at Dolores, whose eyes were glaring at her.

"Dinner? At Tim's? That's funny. He's never asked me over to his house for dinner."

"He's probably just being neighborly," Janis said, hoping to quell the storm before it began.

"Just don't you get too neighborly when you are over there," Dolores said.

"Dolores, Tim is just a good friend of mine," Janis said. "He merely wants me to see some of Oregon before I go back to New York."

Dolores sniffed. "And that can't be too soon as far as I'm concerned. To put it quite bluntly, why don't you pack your things and go back there right away? Haven't enough things happened to you since you've been at Winter House?"

"I'll go when I've finished my work," Janis said in a barely controlled tone of voice. "And not one day before."

Dolores got up from the table. "You may be sorry that you ever came to Winter House."

With that Dolores walked quickly out of the dining room. Janis sat in stunned silence. She wondered now whether it was Dolores who was behind all the irritating things that had happened to her since she had arrived at Winter House. Dolores had such anger built up inside her, anger that was directed toward her.

Needing to get away from Winter House for a while, Janis took a walk after lunch. It was a lovely spring day with a pleasant blue sky.

She found herself following a path she had never used before. It led through some dense woods to a clearing. There Janis found a large rock with a smooth surface on top. She sat on the rock and curled her legs up beneath her.

She just wouldn't let the people at Winter House get her down. She would enjoy her stay here at the house.

Janis glanced around and tried to focus on the awesome beauty that surrounded her. Yet at that moment she could not rid herself of the feeling that she was being watched. Janis scanned the nearby trees and the heavy growth of underbrush in the vain hope that she might be able to make out the watcher.

There was no movement among the pine trees or in the dense undergrowth. She felt that she was becoming slightly paranoid about this whole matter of Winter House.

Janis leaned back and let the sunlight warm her body. It felt good to just relax and not think about the book, the people at Winter House, or any of her problems. Then she stretched out and cushioned her head on her arm. The sun felt so warm that she became drowsy and her eyelids fluttered and then relaxed. She just wanted to sleep, to take a short nap.

When Janis awoke, it was with a start. She had felt a shadow come between herself and the sun. She stirred restlessly and then opened her eyes. Then she sat bolt upright and looked around. Janis half expected to see someone standing near the rock, but there was nobody around. Then she glanced down at the ground near the rock and she saw that the thick grass there had been disturbed as though someone had been standing near her and watching her.

The sudden realization that someone had been that close to her startled Janis. She felt a chilling, quickening fear and decided that she had better get back to the house. She should never have wandered so far from it.

By the time she reached the house, though, she had almost forgotten about the incident.

Instead, she glanced at her watch and decided to take a bath before Tim came by to take her to his place for dinner. She glanced toward the study and decided that she would just leave the sketches in the room until tomorrow. They would be safe there and she would just pick up where she had left off today.

Tim was right on time and when he saw Janis, he

said, "You look lovely. Wait until Loretta sees who I'm bringing to dinner."

"Loretta?"

"She's my cook and general housekeeper. A regular whiz. I don't know how I could have been so lucky to have found her. However, all good things must come to an end. Loretta is leaving me for another man."

By this time they were in Tim's car and he had started the engine.

"Another man?"

Tim sighed. "She's getting married. And her husband doesn't want her to work. At least not for a while anyway."

"How lucky for Loretta," Janis said with a slight chuckle.

"Lucky for her but unlucky for me," Tim said. "You don't know how difficult it is to find someone in Call's Bay to come out here to work."

"You're resourceful," Janis said. "I doubt that you will be very long without help."

"Think so?" Tim said. "I hope you are right."

They talked then until Tim parked the car in front of his house. Once they were inside, he led her to a big, tastefully furnished living room. There was a blazing fire crackling in the oblong off-white fireplace. With its corduroy upholstery and browns and greens, the room looked very casual and very masculine.

"Well, what do you think?" Tim said as he made a sweeping gesture with one arm.

"It's very cozy," Janis said.

"Not like Winter House," Tim said. "A little too small for my needs. What I couldn't do with that house."

At that moment Loretta entered from somewhere off

to the left. She was a short, squat woman with a heavily lined face that came from too much smiling.

Loretta was smiling now as she said, "Dinner's just about ready. So don't you two get into any heavy conversation."

Tim introduced Janis to Loretta. Janis immediately liked the woman.

"Pleased to meet you, Miss Long. I've heard about you. Oh, don't look so surprised. A place as small as Call's Bay has no secrets. You're very pretty. And you look like you got a good head on your shoulders."

They chatted for a few minutes and Tim kidded Loretta about leaving him. It was all very good-natured. Janis felt herself beginning to relax and she knew that she would enjoy the evening.

They ate in a small dining room that was off the living room and Loretta served them a wonderful meal. Janis was thankful that she had had only a salad for lunch. By the time coffee came, she couldn't have eaten another mouthful.

"That was wonderful, Loretta," Janis said as the cook poured coffee into her cup.

"Thanks, Miss Long. It's good to have company in this house. Too bad Mr. Roark waited so long to invite anyone here."

After Loretta had gone, Tim said, "Now you see what I've been talking about. Loretta's one in a million. Only other cook that can beat her is Winnifred."

"But she belongs at Winter House," Janis said and took a sip of the coffee.

"Then I'll just have to buy Winter House if Winnifred won't come here."

Janis giggled. "You aren't serious."

"Dead serious. I'd give just about anything to get my hands on that place. But then I've told you all about that before. If Clifford would just not be so stubborn. However, I'm not licked yet. I don't give up that easily."

Looking at Tim Roark's determined chin, Janis could very well believe that he was telling the truth. Winter House had become an obsession with him. Even though Clifford Green evidently showed no sign of selling the house, Tim was not discouraged. He really meant it when he said that he intended to have the place.

Janis felt the uneasiness she had experienced earlier that day beginning to return. It was just Tim's attitude that brought about the feeling. For her the evening had suddenly taken a sour note.

Tim seemed to sense the change in Janis and he changed the subject. The spell, however, was not regained and Janis was almost relieved when it was time to return to Winter House.

As she got out of the car at the door of Clifford Green's mansion, Tim looked at her and said, "Give me another chance, Janis. It all started out so well."

"I know. It was just me. You may not believe me, but I did have a good time. And Loretta is someone special."

Tim drove off and Janis walked toward the house. She was sorry that the evening had ended up the way it had. But Tim did not seem disappointed or discouraged. So she entered the house with a light tread.

Janis was about halfway up the stairs when she remembered the sketches in the study. Perhaps it would be a good idea not to leave them lying around. She walked briskly back down the stairs. The house was very quiet and it seemed to be mocking her.

She hurried to the study and touched the light switch. Then she gasped as she stared at the desk where she had left the sketches. Someone had viciously torn them up, and pieces of her artwork were scattered all over the desk and floor.

CHAPTER NINETEEN

"Oh, no!" Janis muttered.

Then she picked up the torn pieces of paper and put them down. At first she thought she would cry.

But the tears would not come. Another emotion took over and she became angry. This was just senseless cruelty. Why would anyone be so spiteful?

Janis walked over to the library telephone. It was easy to get Tim's number from the operator.

Loretta answered the phone.

"May I speak to Mr. Roark, please, Loretta. This is Janis Long calling."

"He's busy at the moment, Miss Long. I'll have him call you as soon as he's free. Is anything the matter?"

Janis realized the urgency that was in her voice. She did not want to alarm Loretta since she had just met the woman.

"Just tell him I'd like to speak to him when he has

a minute," Janis said and then hung up.

Slowly Janis went to the study to stare at the mess someone had made of her artwork. She could always redo the sketches, especially since her ideas had been formulated. That would be no problem. It was just the viciousness of the action that bothered her. She walked over to the desk and stooped down to pick up all the pieces of the sketches. After she had gathered them together, she placed them carefully on the desk. This was almost the last straw. Whoever wanted her to leave Winter House really resented her a great deal.

It all had to come to a stop, Janis thought. Somehow she had to get to the bottom of all this.

At that moment the phone rang. Without waiting for either Winnifred or Mary Lee to answer it, Janis hurried to the library and picked up the receiver.

"Hello, Tim?"

"Janis! Loretta said you'd called, that you sounded upset about something. What's going on over there?" Tim's voice sounded calm and reassuring.

"I am upset. Something has happened," Janis said, trying to keep the anger out of her voice.

"Are you all right?"

"Yes, I'm fine. Well, that's not exactly true. I'm very, very angry."

"Try to be calm and tell me all about it," Tim said.

"I'll try. This morning I was doing some sketches for the book. And I left the sketches on the desk in the study. When I came home from your place, I found that someone had torn them up. They're all ripped to pieces."

"That's pretty bad. Sounds as though someone was getting pretty desperate over there. Are you sure you're all right?" Tim said in a concerned tone.

"Physically, I'm fine. Who would want to do this thing, Tim? It must be the same person who left the tape in my room."

There was a pause at the other end of the line. Then Tim said, "I guess that takes care of your work on the book, doesn't it? That's too bad."

"It just slows up the process," Janis said. "I can always redo the sketches. And I have others upstairs. If the person who did this thought it would prevent me from completing my work here, they are sadly mistaken."

"I would come over there, but some business came up that I just can't leave at the moment. Just stay calm and don't do anything foolish. I'll be over there as soon as I can," Tim said, and then he hung up.

Janis stood there for a moment, staring at the instrument in her hand. Then she slowly put the telephone back on its cradle. Tim had told her to stay calm, but how could she with what had happened?

She took some of her torn sketches from the study desk. She needed to confront someone.

Janis found Dolores in the living room idly leafing through a fashion magazine. Dolores glanced up as Janis entered the room and then went back to the magazine.

"Did you have anything to do with this?" Janis said, thrusting the scraps in front of Dolores's face.

"Did I have anything to do with what?" Dolores said in a matter-of-fact voice.

"These are my sketches," Janis said. "Or what's left of them. I'd left them in the study. While I was at Tim's place, somebody tore them up."

"Why would I do something like that?" Dolores said with studied indifference. "Besides, it might have just been somebody's idea of a practical joke,"

"There's nothing funny about destroying my sketches," Janis said.

"Maybe they were doing you a service," Dolores said. "Perhaps it was just a critic who didn't particularly like your work."

Janis was fighting to keep control of her temper. "The critic, as you put it, will have to get used to the idea that I am not easily discouraged. I will sketch again in the study. This hasn't prevented me from completing the book. Or it hasn't succeeded in frightening me away from Winter House."

Dolores looked up from her magazine. "My, my, aren't we getting a little bit melodramatic. Or should I say paranoid? You don't really think that someone is trying to frighten you into leaving Winter House."

Janis decided to speak her mind. It might be the wrong thing to say, but she had to say it. "Are you jealous because I'm seeing Tim Roark, Dolores?"

That did the trick. The haughty look quickly vanished from Dolores's face. Her eyes blazed with anger. "Tim Roark and I are practically engaged. If I were you, I would stay away from him."

"Engaged? Aren't you just being a bit premature? Has he asked you to marry him? And where is the engagement ring? I don't see one on your finger."

Dolores got to her feet and flung the magazine down on the chair. "Just stay away from Tim Roark. That's all I have to say to you."

The tall, statuesque brunette stalked to the door. She paused for a moment and then said over her shoulder,

"I didn't destroy your sketches, but I really think it was a good idea. Too bad I didn't think of it."

With that Dolores left the room. Janis stood there, feeling tired and defeated. She should never have said those things to Dolores, but it was too late now. There was no way in this world that she and Dolores Webster would ever be friends.

Then she walked out of the living room and saw Lucas talking to Dolores. When they saw Janis, their conversation ceased and Dolores walked out of the corridor, leaving Lucas alone.

Lucas made no effort to move as Janis walked toward him. His eyes shifted from Janis's face to what she clutched in her hand.

"I see you made it home from your dinner engagement safe and sound," Lucas said.

"Yes, I did. But maybe I should have stayed here to protect my property."

"Your property?"

"This," Janis said, showing him the shreds of the sketches.

"What is that?"

"It used to be my sketches. I left them in the study today. Somebody tore them. And this is what's left of them!"

Lucas raised one curious eyebrow. "Why are you showing them to me?"

Janis was staring intently into Lucas's face, but it was impassive and did not give away any of his thoughts.

"Did you have anything to do with this?" she asked.

Lucas stared at the scraps of paper and said, "I don't know what you are talking about."

"I'm talking about somebody coming into the study while I was away and deliberately destroying my art-work. And I don't believe that it was just a practical joke."

"Like I said before, Miss Long, maybe you had better leave Winter House. It certainly doesn't seem to agree with you."

"Is that all you have to say?"

Lucas looked somewhere over Janis's head. His mouth was set in a hard, firm line. "I have work to do. If you will excuse me."

Janis was left holding the torn pieces of paper in her hand as Lucas walked away. She wanted to run after him, to try and confront him again for some answer, but she knew that it would be hopeless. Just as it had been hopeless with Dolores.

If either one of them had done this, they certainly would not confess to it. What else had she expected?

Turning, Janis went into the study and dropped the handful of paper onto the desk with the rest of the ruined sketches. She was tempted to make a long distance call to Clifford Green and tell him exactly what had happened, but it was so late back there that she decided to wait until the morning.

As she stood there, she heard a sound from the corridor and she turned to see Mary Lee standing in the doorway.

"What happened in here? Are those your sketches, Janis?"

"What's left of them," Janis said, and then she decided to query Mary Lee. "You didn't see or hear anyone in the study while I was gone, did you, Mary Lee?"

"I'm sorry, but I was busy helping Mom. Then we watched the news on TV. I heard you talking to Mr. Green and I couldn't help but find out what happened."

Janis sighed. "It looks as though our phantom is at it again. Whoever wants me to leave Winter House is certainly making it very plain."

"That's terrible. All of your hard work ruined just like that."

"It's just a temporary setback," Janis said soothingly. "I'll just redo these sketches. That part of it doesn't bother me. It's the maliciousness behind it that bothers me. There's no telling what this person will think up next."

"Can I bring you a cup of coffee?" Mary Lee suggested, and that sounded like a good idea to Janis.

After Mary Lee had gone, Janis found a wastebasket and disposed of the ruined sketches. She picked up the pad, which still contained a few unused sheets, and a determination surged through her. She would not be defeated. Nor would she be driven from Winter House. If anything, this latest episode made her more eager than ever to remain.

After Mary Lee had brought the coffee, they both sat down and had a cup of the hot, bracing liquid.

"What do you do now?" Mary Lee asked after she had taken a sip from her cup.

"Now I just start all over again. I can always use the practice," Janis said in a joking manner.

"Good for you," Mary Lee said. "I didn't think you were the type of person who was easily defeated. Frankly, I wouldn't blame you if you packed your things and left Winter House."

Janis moaned slightly. "Not you too, Mary Lee."

Mary Lee waved one hand frantically. "I didn't mean it that way. I don't want you to go. To tell you the truth, you're the best thing that's happened to Winter House since I've been here. This place can get awfully weird sometimes. Like I've heard footsteps late at night. Somebody goes outside and takes that walk to the cliff. Whoever it is stays there for all hours and then slips back inside the house."

"Have you ever seen who this person is?" Janis asked.

Before Mary Lee could answer, Winnifred came to the door and asked her daughter to help her move something in the kitchen.

After Mary Lee had gone, Janis thought about what the girl had said. What was going on here at Winter House? Had it anything to do with that hideout that Floyd had told her about?

Janis made a decision at that moment, a dangerous decision. She would find that hideout and perhaps it might contain some of the answers to the questions that had arisen since she had come to Winter House.

She hurried to her room and made sure her other sketches were all right. Then she put on a jacket and got out the flashlight that she had found in one of the drawers. As she went down the staircase, she kept watching to see if anyone was around, but she saw neither Lucas nor Dolores.

Outside, the wind had arisen and she buttoned the jacket. The strong breeze tossed her wheat-colored hair into her eyes, but she brushed the strands away with a sweep of her hand. Janis followed the trail that led to the cliff. She knew where the hemlock tree was located.

As she walked she thought about which one of the

people in the house had destroyed her drawings. Had it been Lucas or Dolores? It might have been Jonas, since she hadn't dismissed him as a suspect. Or it could even have been Tim Roark. After all, the sketches were there in the study all afternoon. Tim could have wandered into the house and seen them and for whatever reason decided to destroy them. Janis shivered at that thought. She so desperately did not want it to be Tim Roark.

Nearing the edge of the cliff, she took a side trail that branched off the main path. This pathway was cut parallel to the upper part of the cliff. She turned the flashlight so that she could see this unfamiliar pathway. By now the wind coming in from the sea was cold and her hands were damp from the spray.

Janis kept her eyes on the lone hemlock tree as she walked cautiously along the pathway. Occasionally, she turned to see if she were being followed, but there was nobody on the trail behind her.

Finally, she arrived at a cluster of rocks directly below the tree. Janis turned the light in the direction of the rocks and saw an opening that might have been overlooked if she hadn't known about it.

Pushing aside some underbrush, she crept over the rocks until she found herself inside the cave. With a sweeping motion of her hand, Janis took in this place that Floyd Phillips had told her about. An inner voice told her to turn and run, she was in grave danger.

For a moment Janis was tempted to obey that impulse. Then the flashlight picked up something that caught her attention.

CHAPTER TWENTY

In the corner of the crude makeshift room stood some chairs. Janis moved across the earthen floor to get a closer look at them. She could tell as she neared them that they were antiques. Focusing the light on the backs of the chairs she saw the two bears. Only, this time they were facing each other as she had first seen them in the study. What was going on in here? she wondered.

Casting the light around, she saw a small table in the center of the room and a kerosene lamp resting on top of it. She sniffed the air and there was a faint aroma of varnish in it. In one corner was a pile of rags and some sandpaper and tools.

Going back to the corner, Janis re-examined the two chairs with the bears. Yes, these were the ones that she had seen in the study.

As she stood there, she suddenly got the feeling that

she was not alone in the room. A quick, sudden chill raced down her spine. Slowly Janis turned and she saw a figure standing in the doorway. It was the figure of a man.

"So you've found my little secret," said a familiar voice and Janis raised the flashlight and stared into the face of Lucas Green.

"How did you know I was in here?" Janis asked shakily.

"I followed you, of course," Lucas said.

Then he walked over to the table and, taking a match from his pocket, lighted the kerosene lamp. "Take a good look around, Miss Long. Since you are so very curious about things here at Winter House."

Janis merely stared at Lucas. His eyes seemed to bore holes in her.

"What is all this, Lucas?" she finally said, making a quick gesture with her hand. "Those two chairs are from the study, aren't they?"

"That's right. And underneath that tarp in the corner you will find an end table from the upstairs corridor and a small desk from one of the guest rooms."

"What are they doing here?" Janis asked, not taking her eyes off Lucas's face.

"Waiting for a buyer. Those particular chairs with the bear carvings will bring me quite a tidy sum of money. And just in time, I might add. There are certain bills that have to be paid."

Janis finally took her eyes off Lucas and looked once again at the two chairs. "But they were in the study. Only, the bears were not facing each other like they are now."

Lucas made a clucking sound with his mouth. "I

know. A little slip on my part. I will have to remake one of the chairs."

"Remake?" Janis asked.

"Of course. That's what I've been doing over the past year. I have been duplicating the antiques in my dear father's house and selling the originals to a man who, shall we say, doesn't ask questions as to where they come from."

Janis stared at Lucas. "Why?"

"Why! I needed the money, that's why. I've always been good with my hands and so I stumbled onto this idea of reproducing the antiques at Winter House. My father certainly doesn't give me enough money to live on. It's really all his fault."

Janis could see that Lucas's reasoning was all twisted. She could hardly believe what she was hearing.

"You've been selling all of your father's antiques. But you can't get away with that," Janis said.

Lucas laughed. "Can't I? Nobody knows the difference. Except maybe you. When you were sketching the chairs in the study to be used in the book, I knew that my father would notice the difference when he saw my mistake in reproducing the bears."

"Then it was you who destroyed my sketches."

"Of course. I figured you would get discouraged and at least leave those chairs out of the illustrations," Lucas said, staring at Janis with hard, unblinking eyes.

"What about the tape I found in my room when I first arrived here?"

"I put it there. It was a plan to frighten you into leaving. But that didn't work the way I thought it would. You are a very stubborn and determined woman, Miss Long. I also tried to push you down the stairs.

Too bad you moved when you did."

Janis was clutching the flashlight tightly in her hand. It was the only weapon she had to defend herself with. There was no telling what lengths Lucas would go to when he finally decided that she knew too much.

"Then you climbed up the wall and took the tape recorder that night?"

"A piece of cake. All I needed was a ladder, which I borrowed. But even that did not seem to discourage you. So I followed you that night you went to the beach. You seemed very frightened when I chased you up the path. Frightened enough to finally leave Winter House. There again I was wrong."

Janis began to move slowly away from Lucas, but she knew that she had to keep him talking until she could make it to the entrance of the workshop. She might have a chance if she got out ahead of Lucas. But Lucas seemed to sense what she was thinking and he moved to block her escape.

"Today when I was asleep on that rock, somebody awakened me. It must have been you."

"That was a mistake. I could have very easily gotten rid of you then. But you awoke before I had the chance," Lucas said, his eyes glistening.

"And all that time I thought it might be Floyd Phillips," Janis said. "At first, anyway."

"He was fortuitous. A stroke of luck. If he hadn't been found out, I could rely on him to take the blame for driving you away from Winter House. Too bad that interfering Tim Roark caught him with you."

"Is that why you did all those things?" Janis said. "To drive me away from Winter House?"

Again Lucas said, "It just wouldn't do for you to be

poking your nose around here. I knew that it would be a matter of time before you stumbled onto something. And when I saw you sketching those chairs, I suddenly realized the mistake I had made in reproducing them."

"Lucas, you know what you did was wrong. Why don't you just tell your father? Maybe something can be worked out."

At the mention of his father, Lucas became agitated. His eyes narrowed into slits. "My father. He's such a great man. Always expecting great things out of me. But I'm not like him. Why should I work when he has all that money? He expected too much from me."

Janis knew that she had made a mistake in mentioning Clifford Green. If she could just think of something, some words that would get Lucas's twisted mind off his father. But she was speechless. Then she remembered the flashlight in her hand.

She calculated the distance between herself and the entrance of the workshop and then turned the light fully upon Lucas's face. He was temporarily blinded by the glare, and Janis ran to the entrance.

She had a few moments' advantage and she took it, scrambling over the rocks and through the brush that grew around the entrance. But she was not quick enough. As she got to her feet, she felt strong hands grasp her shoulders.

"You're not going anywhere," Lucas said harshly. "I've told you too much. You can't be trusted now."

Janis was struggling with Lucas, and they got nearer and nearer to the edge of the cliff. Below, Janis could hear the terrifying sound of the waves.

She screamed for help once, but that took too much energy that she could use to ward off Lucas. Meanwhile, Lucas edged her toward the rim of the cliff.

Janis was weakening. She was no match for Lucas. A sudden gust of wind struck them and they both teetered for a moment on the rim of the cliff. Janis closed her eyes to blot out what she felt was about to happen.

At that moment she heard a shout and Lucas released his grip on her. Janis opened her eyes and saw Lucas struggling with someone. It was all very fast and confusing. Then she saw that the other person was Tim Roark. Lucas put up a good fight, but Tim was the stronger one.

In a few minutes, it was all over. Lucas lay unconscious on the ground and Tim hurried over to Janis. He stretched out his arms and she willingly let him hold her.

"Darling, are you all right? I had to wait for the right time. He didn't hurt you, did he?"

Janis snuggled in his strong arms, welcoming the comfort of his embrace.

In a few moments he released her, and she said, "I'm fine. Lucas was the one who was behind all that's been happening to me at the house. He's been selling the antique furniture and replacing it with fakes."

"How do you know all this?"

"Floyd told me about this hiding place he had found. He said it was full of furniture and things. So I came here to find out for myself. I thought maybe I could discover something about what has been going on at Winter House."

"That was a dangerous thing to do," Tim said. "You should have waited for me."

"I know. But at the time I just didn't know who I could trust."

Tim tilted her chin with his hand. "Do you know now?"

"Yes," Janis replied as Tim bent his head and gently brushed her lips with his. The kiss was brief, but it answered a question that had been building in Janis's heart.

"You go back to the house and call the authorities," Tim said. "I'll bring Lucas with me when he comes around. Okay?"

"Okay," Janis said and she reluctantly walked back to the house.

All the way back she kept thinking about Lucas and how mixed up he was. He really needed some professional help. She hoped that his father and the authorities would not be too hard on him.

After she had telephoned the sheriff, she waited for a moment or two and then made a decision. Clifford Green must be told about what had been going on here at Winter House. Taking a deep breath, Janis dialed long distance.

Clifford Green answered the phone and Janis told him as calmly as possible about Lucas and his problems.

"I'll be on the next plane," Clifford Green said before he hung up.

By the time the sheriff arrived, Tim had brought Lucas into the house. The sheriff listened while Tim and Janis explained everything.

In the end Lucas was taken away and Dolores said, "This is just too unbelievable. All of this happening right before my eyes and I didn't see any of it."

"Why don't you go to bed, Janis," Tim said. "I'll be back in the morning to check up on you."

Janis had to admit that she was dead tired. It had been a harrowing experience and now she felt drained.

As Janis walked out of the room she heard Tim say to Dolores, "I want to have a few words with you."

All Janis could think about was getting to her room and trying to get some sleep. She knew that tomorrow would be another trying day.

The next day Clifford Green arrived in a rented car. He had been to the sheriff's office and he appeared pale and haggard. He listened quietly as Janis told him everything.

Occasionally, he would look at her with great concern in his eyes. When she finished, he said, "I know this has been a terrible experience for you, Janis. Probably I should never have asked you to come here. But in a way I'm glad you did. I would never have learned about Lucas and what he's been doing if it wasn't for you."

"I'm very sorry about that, Clifford," Janis said.

Clifford waved a hand. "Lucas and I had a long talk. He needs help, professional psychiatric help. I guess I'm at fault too for expecting too much of him. But I would like to ask a favor of you, Janis."

Janis nodded.

"I can't blame you if you refuse after all you've been through. But I am asking you not to press charges against Lucas. I'm not pressing charges. Oh, I intend to make him work and repay what he got from the sale of those antiques. That is, after he gets himself straightened out. What do you say?"

Janis thought for a moment and then said, "Of course, I won't, Clifford. I realize Lucas wasn't in his right mind when he did all these things. You have my word."

Clifford Green breathed a deep sigh of relief.

"But I will ask for more time for my drawings. It seems that my work has been interrupted," Janis said lightly.

Clifford Green smiled at her and agreed with her request.

That afternoon Janis was coming out of the kitchen when she saw Dolores descending the staircase. She was carrying a suitcase in one hand.

"I'm leaving," Dolores said. "This house is beginning to get on my nerves. So I guess this is good-by, Miss Long."

"This is so unexpected," Janis said.

"Not really," Dolores replied. "The only reason I was staying on was because of Tim Roark. But we had a nice long chat last night. And it seems we have less in common than I thought. He doesn't think much of my friends and I certainly wouldn't give them up for him."

Janis didn't know what to say, so she kept silent.

"My taxi should be here by now. I'll send the driver up for my other things," Dolores said as she started for the door. Before she left, she turned and said, "Tim Roark is all yours, dear. As a matter of fact, here comes the young Frank Lloyd Wright now."

Dolores walked out, leaving the door open. Janis stood by the staircase as Tim entered. For a moment, he was blinded by the darkness in the corridor. Then he saw Janis and she hurried to him and his outstretched arms.

"This may be too early to say, but I'm going to anyway," Tim said.

"What?"

"That I love you, Janis Long. I have from the moment you mistakenly came to my house the day you arrived."

"I don't think it's too early to hear those words," Janis said. "Not too early at all."

Then Tim leaned down and his kiss was urgent but tender. For Janis the trouble at Winter House had finally ended. Tim had given her a bright promise of an even brighter future.